The Road
to
Kaibara

Gbanabom Hallowell

The Road to Kaibara

Copyright © 2015 by Gbanabom Hallowell
All rights reserved.

ISBN: 978-99910-54-01-8

Sierra Leonean Writers Series
c/o Mallam O. & J. Enterprises
120 Kissy Road, Freetown; Warima, Sierra Leone
Publisher: Prof. Osman Sankoh (Mallam O.)
www.sl-writers-series.org
publisher@sl-writers-series.org
writersseries.sl@gmail.com

for Lamin Gbanabom Sankoh
a truly friendly family

1

This is a story inside a story. My name is Desmond Johnson and I've been in exile for thirty years now. I suddenly developed an intense urge to return home to Kaibara. However, my muse told me that I first needed to fill the gap of absence by seeking a narrator to inform me about happenings in Kaibara since I left for exile.

The narrator I saught prepared me to accept that his account was going to be a long story. A man who has been gone for thirty years would need to know not only the history he did not witness but the roles he did not play leading to why his history is what it is.

According to the narrator, this account is a combination of what I already know of the political history of Kaibara and what I have missed these thirty years. The opening account was delivered in a big sea vessel in the middle of the Atlantic, an appropriate location separating the land of my birth from the land of my exile.

He looked deeply into my eyes and began:

In the dry season of 1986 the second president of Kaibara since independence announced by radio that he had failed the nation. Kaibarans struggled to understand what side of the bed he had got up on that morning. His announcement came four years before the war broke out and five before the coup that drove him from the seat of power.

A young captain in the beleaguered army had marched from the battlefront two hundred and fifty miles from the border town of Radu to the capital of RoMarong and overthrew the president, the commander who had sent him to war.

The first reaction to the president's broadcast came from a man who, with a baton in hand, hopped about under the cotton tree which stood in the center of town. He called for the president to be treated in the perspective of his broadcast. He raced from under the cotton tree and looked at the sun as though it was behind schedule for an appointment they both had set.

Pointing his finger at it, he challenged its burning rays.

"*Ra!*" he said.

It was little more than a gasp with hardly any esoteric propinquity.

The man stood six feet five inches. The mop of hair on his head ran down his jaws, all the way to his bushy, gray-haired cheeks. Occasionally, he passed a brush through it. He loved to have his hair hanging over his chin. He was meticulous enough to pick out and uproot any black follicle that popped up in it. It had to be gray and silver all the way, he would say. He carried

2

a Socratic posture about him. His tatters hung loosely on his body, free of any patches, proudly proclaiming his hunchback.

Everyone called him Borbor Pain, and most people believed that he was mad. Going round the cotton tree three times and coming to the full view of a small crowd that idled around him, Borbor Pain squatted. He thrust his left hand forward, indicating that he wanted passage to the end of the street.

The crowd parted, and within seconds he was crisscrossing the traffic.

Dipping into his tatters, he brought out a dilapidated radio. Looking around cautiously like an animal suspicious of danger in the heart of a jungle, he leaped into the air, mindless of the flowing traffic. He stood still in the middle of the street and stared at the pedestrians as though he expected them to engage in something other than their normal going about.

He then returned to his audience.

Unprovoked, he told them they ought to be ashamed of themselves if they had no stand-by-me radios in their possessions. He reminded them that he was not referring to their big furniture gramophones they had left behind in their homes, whose bottoms had to be fired by electricity, which their government was not prepared to provide for them, even if they paid all the taxes in the world.

According to Borbor Pain, real radios were the ones to take to all places one went because only radios that could be carried about protected one in what he called "these turbulent times."

"In this day of our Lord, a radio is a political condom!" he shouted.

He hollered to his audience again to treat the president in the perspective of his broadcast! However, no one in the crowd knew what he was talking about. He told them how much he pitied them for not bothering to be alarmed over presidential blunders such as the one he had just heard broadcast over his radio.

The audience burst into a frenzy of laughter.

He was finished with them, *those doubting Thomases.* He beat his breasts three times and left the crowd wondering as he walked toward the marketplace.

At the marketplace he attracted greater attention because there, with a staggering display of candor, he accompanied his demand for the president to be treated in the perspective of his broadcast.

No sooner was he identified as the familiar man under the cotton tree than people began returning to their personal concerns, waving a backhand flag at his ranting.

Still they had already been struck by his utterance.

"Is he not the madman under the cotton tree?" one woman inquired trying not to pay attention to him. "He's always got something new!"

"Did you say 'a madman'?" someone questioned.

Even among those against whom he railed, not everyone thought Borbor Pain was a mad man. He was largely perceived of as one of those religious zealots known to be clad in rags along lonely paths, beating their breasts and chanting in parables long before the war broke out. However, when they looked about to

4

see what Borbor Pain would do or say next, they saw that he was already lost in the crowd.

The president's broadcast had been made that afternoon without warning. Rumors of it had started like a comet that had passed unnoticed by most, but as the day faded around the square, Borbor Pain could be heard in drifting crowds again calling for the president to be treated in the perspective of his broadcast.

His words drifted on the wind.

Like a scent, it went down the marketplace and resurfaced in multiple versions. Some maintained that if indeed the president had uttered that he had failed the nation, he had certainly meant his words as some sort of rhetorical figure of speech, such as a wise man might use.

To others, the president had only been quoting his detractors who sat in the comfort of their homes conjuring doom for the nation. Still others felt that, after all, it was time the president realized he had really failed the nation.

With the high cost of living, which had made it difficult for parents to provide square meals for their children, hadn't the country become a victim of the dump of expired European foodstuffs that kept sending able-bodied men to their deathbeds as quickly as a famine?

Were diseases not taking their toll on the population?

Hadn't children been deprived of much needed education because parents couldn't afford the fees?

Were men and women not idling about for lack of jobs?

Borbor Pain's advice mixed with the rumored news. It had followed groups into crowded buses, along footpaths, into mosques and churches, and into media houses, wherever the tributaries of survival flowed with a crowd.

Word about the broadcast suddenly echoed in dark alleys. Not many people had heard the news when it had been first aired that afternoon. Afternoons were not proper times to listen to radios because people were busy searching for their daily bread.

Ten o'clock at night was the usual time the Government owned broadcasting service went over daily presidential events, and then it went over them again before the station shut down for the day at 12:00 a.m. A final broadcast would be set for 9:00 a.m. the following day, and that would be the last time for the business of educating the people for one day on the relentless efforts of their government to provide for their welfare and protection.

That evening, 10 p.m. came and went with the indecipherable jazz of a little known Duke Ellington in the air. Twelve a.m. struck with a somewhat inadvertent link with the BBC.

By the morning, many people believed that the crap was one of the usual tall tales fit only for the early hours of April fool's day. The morning radio had mentioned nothing about the speech. Instead it had played a jamboree of musical escapades featuring the top BBC and VOA musical charts. The only hope for anyone

6

wishing to learn about the president's speech was the independent print media. The next morning a tabloid carried a headline about the confessional broadcast:

PRESIDENTIAL BLUNDER CONFESSED ON STATE RADIO!

It ended with an embarrassing exclamation mark that bewitchingly attracted everyone's attention.

So it was true after all.

At one open street, the paper sold like hot cakes. The line to purchase one grew longer and longer as the morning progressed. The demand soared and so did the price of the paper. The crowd was boisterous.

"Ready the exact money, I have no change!" the happy, sweating vendor kept warning.

"Boy, don't sell more than one paper to one individual!" an impatient customer shouted.

"One paper for you and one paper for me so that we can all get a copy!" a refrain followed.

"That is what we call equal rights!" another shouted from the back of the line.

"Equal rights exist in this country? You are dreaming!" another put in.

"At least us the poor should practice it among ourselves," another said.

"Woman, steady, it is this bustling about that has suddenly hiked the cost of the paper!"

"This is a photocopy, don't you have the original? This doesn't read properly"

"Are we not currently ruled by a government of photocopycracy?" a disheveled bystander put in.

The crowd burst out laughing.

"Make sure you buy only from me. Tricky people may want to cheat you with stale issues of the same paper!"

The vendor was enjoying his sales.

The queue was long and the wind was swaying it. Occasionally it surged forward but was thrown backward with such force that it was flung sideways and split in the middle. Another line attempted to run up to the vendor, but it was vehemently opposed and those in the new line laid over the original line to secure places in it.

It was then that the wind came in its full force. Huge thunderclaps were accompanied by smaller blasts. Suddenly a small group of soldiers entered from every corner of the street. Once in sight, they raised their guns skyward and released a barrage of shots that sent everyone seeking refuge.

The obtuse vendor knelt to gather the newspapers his customers had dropped about. When the soldiers approached him, he was commanded to hand over every one of his newspapers.

The vendor shivered before them.

Two soldiers reached for the papers under his armpits. He attempted to explain that he was a mere vendor who eked out his living by selling newspapers. Such raids were not strange on vendors of his day. To people observing from a distance, it was not clear why he didn't just shut up and run away.

One of the soldiers shouted for him to obey and not complain.

A swift kick to his groin sent him writhing on the ground. Before he found strength to massage the spot, another one landed on his face. He saw stars. A third one cutting across his chest quickly followed. With the butt of a gun a fourth soldier struck him on his head.

The vendor gasped, brought himself up to his knees, before contorting in front of the soldier who had made the last assault. The soldier avoided the vendor's cat-bulged eyes, and a little cowed by the result of his assault he pulled back his gun.

The vendor boy released everything in his grip. It was rather like everything dropped from his grip. His hands had first flown into the air before they descended without control. Noticing that he was only a teenager, one of the soldiers began to ask how a young boy like him got mixed up in such a dangerous trade. As if in response to his question, the vendor spat up blood and some more ran down his nose. Languidly, he fell to the ground and remained still.

The soldiers left him there and walked away with the newspapers in their possession.

Borbor Pain was watching the event from under the cotton tree. He took his eyes off the scene only after the soldiers had walked away. He returned to his copy of the newspaper, which, in fact, had only flashed the headline as a teaser. There was no story on the matter. There was merely the promise that the story would be treated in full in the weekend edition.

9

How was anyone to have handled the president's remark? The president's cabinet had not prepared for it. The press still lacked the proper background for its columns. Borbor Pain continued to tell whoever cared to listen that the entire episode was a presidential transgression, a stigma that dwarfed that of President Nixon in the great nation of America.

The government continued to keep its lips sealed. Already a teenage newspaper vendor was dead, and rumor had it that the editor of that particular paper was already in hiding. Later the rumor circulated that he too had been killed.

Other newspaper offices were ransacked in what the police called a search for subversive documents. An insurrection was reported in a corner of RoMarong City, emanating from an argument about the presidential confession. It had taken the lives of a pregnant woman, a policeman, and a teenager. Reports on the radio called it a family feud that had claimed the lives of some of its members and sadly also that of a dutiful policeman.

Regardless of all the bloodshed, on Monday, a clandestine newspaper with a strange name dedicated all its pages to the presidential speech. A fearless editorial ran on the front-page.

The editorial continued by narrating the atrocities of the government. It described the corruption of the president and his cabinet, characterizing them as a boys club. The editorial took to task what it called a rubber-stamping parliament that had abused the confidence its people had placed in it.

The paper called for an overhaul of the entire judiciary system, which it said stank more and more as time went on and already carried unfathomable sins in depriving the defenseless poor of their justice. It called for the restoration of political pluralism, fresh elections, arrest of the president and his team, and a lifelong ban on their political careers.

The newspaper had enjoyed such a wide subterranean circulation that by midday only light photocopies of it could be found around the streets. However, a clean and original copy surfaced in the hands of Borbor Pain. He read every page of it.

At 8:30 p.m., the usual national news program on the radio was interrupted. The announcer apologized to her listeners and prepared them for a special broadcast by the Honorable Minister of Information.

When the minister came on the air, he went straight to the point.

In his address he observed that the government had been made aware of certain unpatriotic persons who were embarking on a campaign to discredit it. The minister denied that his president had, at any time, in any place, and in any circumstance, broadcast that he had failed the nation. He said the government would not allow unpatriotic elements supported by some irresponsible foreign governments through their embassies or high commissions to disrupt the daily activities of peace loving Kaibarans. According to the minister, the government already had in its custody a few of these elements, and that they were currently helping the police with its investigation.

11

In conclusion, the minister admonished all peace loving Kaibarans to go about their business, secure in the knowledge that there was and would always be a government in place to protect their interest.

"Long live the president! Long live the state!"

Borbor Pain did not believe in killing insects. Once, when he had inadvertently stepped on an ant, he carefully picked it up with his index finger. Realizing that the ant was still alive, he carried it to the cotton tree. Placing it on the bark of the giant tree, he spoke softly to it and told it the secret that resided at the top of the tree.

As though the insect understood him and wanted to find out for itself, it stretched its legs, cleaned them with its proboscis, and left for the journey up the cotton tree.

Later that year after witnessing thousands of ants transporting their food to the top of the tree, Borbor Pain explained to anyone who cared to listen to him that he had saved humanity through his kindness to a little ant. He then declared himself a vegetarian.

When the broadcast ended, Borbor Pain plucked the radio from his ears in time to avoid the anachronistic national anthem. He hated to listen to impractical things. Still in his unshakable posture, he cast his eyes onto the thick branches above him where he noticed he beheld the president in the nude.

The president was attempting to hold on to a branch. His face was sour and didn't have the distinct features of a human being. He began swinging from branch to branch like a monkey that was trying to elude a hungry lion. Covered in a slimy substance, each branch undermined the president's grip. Finally, he did, however, find a branch upon which he was able to rest. He plucked leaves from it to cover his nudity. He plucked the leaves until there was not one left.

In its anger the branch shook hard and oozed more of the slimy substance. The president was all dressed up now in leaves, but soon he began losing his grip again. His legs slid off the branch and his hands, having no power to grasp the slimy limb, slid with him.

Borbor Pain thought he was actually seeing the president falling on him; so, he quickly sprang from where he was lying and sought refuge a distance away. When he looked around him, he hoped to see the president's piggish body sprawled on the ground, but he found only an empty spot. He rubbed his eyes with the back of his hands and looked up the tree and saw no one. Neither was there any slimy substance on the branches. The tree was as calm as the day. He muttered to himself and soon allowed the whole incident to pass.

Apparently, it was one of his visions again.

Borbor Pain carried with him that morning an infinite anger. He expressed it in murmur, "You may fall and fall and fall, but you can't fall here, no, not here, Mr. failed President, not on me." He took his radio and stepped from under the cotton tree that had been home to him since—he didn't want to recall that now.

2

It was a hot sunny day in RoMarong City and the year 1986 was just about to wrap up and disappear forever. Grabo Burnah had promised his wife he would stay at home that day. The two of them agreed to settle in with a spicy dish of rice and cassava leaves. They told their three children they too would not be going to school. The children danced about happily thanking their parents for being so kind to them.

Grabo, a senior executive member of the Petty Traders Association, had backed his chairman's emergency proposal for the rapid response action. His wife never trusted him with his promises about taking a break from his business. Grabo paid all his attention to his trading and wanted every profit to provide for his family, so staying at home that day carried with it a heavy burden.

While his wife cooked and his children played about the house, he stood in a chair at the front door from where he monitored the outdoor activities. He could see every corner of the street. The day was passing along without incident. Two of his friends who worked in government offices passed by and briefly spoke with him, but neither acted strangely or mentioned any expected disturbances.

Grabo didn't remember ever taking a vacation or a day off from his business except when he was ill. He always said that a vacation was meant for successful people, and not for him who lived a hand-to-mouth life. As he dozed off in his chair, he dreamed that he saw himself in his stall showing fine ladies' dresses to a woman who had opened her bag, but returned the bundle of money inside it, having decided against buying the dress. When Grabo choked in his sleep and awakened, he sprang from his chair. It was only a dream. But no—it was not just a dream!

He was missing something.

Sitting back with his head up high and nodding in agreement to something that he had quickly turned over in his mind, he rose from the chair. At the back of the house he heard his children playing *akra* and the happy voice of his wife singing *bondo* in the kitchen. Grabo walked stealthily to his room, put on jeans and a T-shirt, and stole out of the compound.

Although they agreed in the emergency meeting not to display their wares, many of the traders had gone out to sit in front of their empty stalls monitoring the pulse of

15

the day in order to determine if the following day would be good for business.

They soon spotted Borbor Pain approaching from the food shop. He carried his radio in his hand. Taunting him was mostly a source of pleasure for the traders. They shouted his name, but upon hearing their outburst of excitement, he quickly put his radio inside his tatters and threw his head up the sky.

"*Ra!*" he shouted.

The outburst of the traders continued. However, Borbor Pain, with his head up high and his hands folded behind him, wove his way among them to make it to his tree. He always wanted a morning rest after breakfast.

"What do we treat in perspective today?" they tempted him.

Borbor Pain ignored them and moved on.

"Where is your stand-by-me? Shouldn't you carry it with you?" the crowd of traders taunted him.

In other circumstances when asked about his radio, Borbor Pain would have quickly removed it from his tatters and flashed it in the air for all to see. This time, however, all he did was say aloud, "Knowledge is power!"

"Where is your worth, madman? Why not tell us how much you admire the president now that the government has denied all you said you heard on your radio?"

Admire the president? Are these people so vulnerable as to admire senseless, mouth-gabbling policies characterized by lies?

He was provoked.

"You must be ashamed of yourselves!" he found himself saying to them. "When do you find time to read between the lines of your lives? Do you have time? By day you are lying to your sisters to eat their food and by night you are hanging around the wives of your neighbors."

The traders burst out laughing.

Street hawkers squeezed into the crowd with their wares to have a peep. A certain woman forced her way into the crowd too. She was loosely dressed in a multicolored *gara* with a high head-tie on her head. It was Grabo's wife. Discovering that her husband had sneaked out of the house, she had left to search for him after finishing her cooking. Now she was searching for her husband in the crowd listening to Borbor Pain.

"Don't many of you pay attention to foolish things whenever you are demanded by serious matters? On Election Day do you not ignore your votes and follow after financial notes?"

The laughter roared louder than before and was followed by applause. People began peering from their vehicles to look into the dense crowd.

Ra stood directly over Borbor Pain. Its burning rays moistened the thick crust of dirt on his body. He didn't attempt to wipe his soaked face because he liked the salty taste of his sweat that settled between his lips.

"Where are they who talk about fasting? Aren't your minds grieving for the slow things?"

The crowd went wild again.

"Don't clap for me like you clapped for your president when he said it all on the radio in effect that

17

from that moment every Kaibaran wasn't thinking right. Therefore, he was changing you all, not me, from being God's children to being a dog's children.

The laughter roared long and loud, ringing into the air.

"No one shall refer to him or herself as a Kaibaran any longer. There will be no such thing as Kaibarans anymore!"

"Like in South Africa!" someone shouted.

"Yes, like in South Africa! Only this is worse! Black on Black!" Borbor Pain mechanically responded. "And do you know why this is going to be so?" he asked the crowd which jubilantly responded that they didn't know why.

"Well I'll tell you," he paused. "They are planning to sell the country."

"To what?" the crowd, trying to beat the noise, shouted.

"To sell the country to the Americans; and the leaders plan to share the money among themselves."

The crowd didn't laugh this time.

A certain fear hung over it.

Finally one woman said, "It's true, oh, us the poor!"

The crowd became boisterous as murmurs of support rang out.

"Don't you see one thing here?" Borbor Pain continued. "The leader confessed his sins on national radio to quicken the sale to the Americans."

The crowd agreed vehemently.

Then suddenly, in the brief moment of a pause by the crowd, a clap thundered in the sky like a volcano.

Soldiers carrying AK47 assault rifles indiscriminately shot into the crowd. People fell to the ground, blood gushing from their wounds. The roar of guns continued, competing with the screams of fear and pain. Then arrests were made. Questions about who the ringleaders were became a salutation.

About fifty people were already in custody with two soldiers pointing guns at them, threatening to shoot them all dead unless they identified the ringleaders. Some of the arrested people pointed at the direction of Borbor Pain.

"It was that madman stirring trouble," they said.

"Stirring what trouble?" the soldiers questioned.

"He was making fun of the president."

"What about the president?"

"He was making fun of his last broadcast to the nation."

"Is there anything funny about it?" And you, standing here calling this fellow a madman? Come here, all of you; and as for you, fellow, your maddening days are over. We have more fun in store for you. We know how to make madmen *real* mad."

A violent hand lifted Borbor Pain from the ground and sent his whole body flying in the air at an unimaginable speed. His head hit against a piece of metal that sounded a gong in the big black hole. His vision blotted out.

Years before the war broke out Dembapa Prison remained the only colonial legacy protected and regularly maintained in Kaibara. Built high and mighty in the heart of RoMarong City, its architecture suggested that the British didn't compromise with native criminals who coughed and complained about the colonial profits channeled to Europe via crouching trains and lugubrious sea vessels.

Even a man as choleric as Bai Bundeh, a feared nineteenth century tribal chief, was not spared the wrath of the British Lords. Native colonial criminals were punished, and, if subdued at all, were reformed in a hard way before being reintegrated into society.

However, only a few years into independence, many Kaibarans perished in the Dembapa Prison. They suffered the mingling of their daily lives on slabs wet from their excrement and blood. They ate food indistinguishable from vomit and served in unhygienic bowls. Locked in a world of stench and darkness, their whipped corpses were abandoned on urine covered floors of the corridors to die, after which their bodies were handcuffed together and thrown into mass graves left open for vultures to scavenge on. Prisoners of conscience suffered even worse fates.

The *Black Mariah* truck drove through the metal gates of the prison and sped to the extreme end of the compound, hooting irritatingly along its way. Prison guards sprang from every corner. In their brown khakis, they paced back and forth like mechanical toys. Inmates were always locked down when new ones were brought in, especially when the arrivals were considered potentially dangerous.

The story was told that one day some new arrivals were brought in hurriedly while inmates were scattered about the compound for exercises. According to law, no inmate was allowed to move about freely when new prisoners were brought in, but on that day, there had been no time to return them to their cells.

The new arrivals had just been swept up in an impromptu police raid and there was little advance warning of their pending arrival at the prison. Taking advantage of the small number of wardens on duty at the time, the inmates had teamed with the arrivals to overpower their captors, tied them up, flung open the metal gates, and escaped in the *Black Mariah* later found abandoned in some remote woods.

This time the wardens were alert. Even off-duty officers had been urgently called in to work that day.

Dembapa Prison was at its busiest.

Already the cells overflowed with inmates. Everyone in the country knew about the one hundred and twelve students languishing in the prison cells. Authorities had been tipped about the new dangers arising on college campuses. Students were reportedly seen gathering late at night with lighted candles in their hands and listening to lectures by strange people who looked like nomadic horsemen.

Borbor Pain and thirteen others stepped out of the truck in cuffs. While Borbor Pain's spirit remained high, the others appeared haggard, confused, and defeated. The wardens conducted a routine search on their bodies and ordered them to squat in front of him, in case they carried weapons in their anuses.

They were ordered to sit in one corner of the room. An officer came from nowhere, and stooped in front of the arrivals. Seizing Borbor Pain by the leg, he removed his shoes from him. Borbor Pain looked at the officer blankly and instantly cooperated.

The officer then proceeded to another prisoner who quickly pulled his legs back and murmured something. The officer merely smiled at him and asked his name.

"Grabo Burnah."

The warden said, "You are new in here. Every prisoner goes through this. This is Dembapa Prison. You don't need your shoes if you are going to be lodged in here."

"Lodged in here did you say? I haven't done anything wrong. If anything it is this madman who must bear the brunt alone," said Grabo Burnah, sweating heavily.

"I wish it were my business to listen to that. I'm only performing my duty," the officer again reached for his leg.

"But you have no right to take our shoes off our feet. We need them every hour we are here. You can't take mine off!" Grabo insisted.

"Do you know you are inside Dembapa Prison? This is not the same place you see when you are outside of it." the officer thundered. Suddenly Grabo looked like a drowning man.

Another arrival whispered something to him. Staring back at him, Grabo grumbled weakly and stretched his legs. The officer continued his work until he reached the last arrival.

"You can always have them back when you leave," the officer looked about before adding. "That's not always true, though. I have seen men, giants and lords, walk out of here barefoot, but I'll see to it that you have your belongings if you behave."

He began to walk away. "And another thing," he said, looking directly into the eyes of Grabo. "Try hard not to anger the wardens in here. They can be real nasty. They are gods all by themselves."

"Gods!" another arrival remarked after the officer had disappeared through a door. "If these are cruel gods then I wonder what we are all in here."

Grabo bowed his head and began to sob. He told the man who had whispered into his ear that he was worried about his wife who had come looking for him in the crowd. The others tried to sooth him, telling him to take heart. They reasoned with him that his wife could well have escaped and gone home, but that if she had been captured, she would currently be in the same building with the group of other women.

Grabo glanced through his fellow arrivals again, but there was no one among them that he knew. It seemed that he was the only unlucky one among his trading colleagues to have been captured.

He was still sobbing when suddenly he felt cold water running down his head! The others had been sprayed too. Two or three of them choked and began to cough. More water splashed on them. The wardens then tore the prisoners' clothes from their bodies. Not even their pants were spared. They tried to resist but being cuffed, they could do very little. It was not hard to overcome them. Soon they sat naked on the cold slab.

A few minutes later the wardens stood aside to let a neatly dressed bespectacled, older man walk through. He was the commissioner.

"Welcome to Dembapa Prison!" said the commissioner.

He had a black staff under his armpits. His shoe studs sounded loud on the slab. "Now you are all going to follow me to a room where you will wait until each one of you has made a statement. Our duty here is to see that you are protected from the mob you have angered so badly out there. Don't ask me when you are getting out of here. It is not for me to say. And I must say this, that I can't stand disrespect and disobedience. I repeat, I can't—*cannot*—put up with disrespect and disobedience. I hope I have—"

"But our clothes," one man said. "Where are they? We can't go—"

In the eerie silence that followed, three wardens reached out and registered three heavy blows to the jaws, chest, and stomach of the man who spoke before shoving his head against the wall.

"I hope I have made myself clear," said the commissioner. He continued as though nothing had interrupted him. He turned around to the salutations of his men as though to refill his authority.

"Now I can see that you are getting adjusted. Let me introduce myself to you," the commissioner said. "My name is Dunstant Omotayo Melvin Coker. I am in charge here, and by here I mean this place, Dembapa Prison. Five years ago it pleased the president of our great Republic, and it continues to please him each year,

24

to appoint me commissioner of the Dembapa Prison. Day in day out, I'm in charge. Present in body or only in spirit, I rule this great empire. "I meet people like you every day; I believe some of you have been here before in like circumstances. I have been honored with the hard task of taming four point five million Kaibarans, which of course excludes the president, Grand Commander of the Armed Forces, and all his fine members of cabinet.

"Talking about the president, I should note here that the president has too many heavenly blessings for cursed roaches like you to cause him any harm. That must go into your heads in case you wish to withhold any information regarding other cursed Kaibarans, embassies or high commissions, military officers, journalists, organizations, and devils like yourselves who sent you out into the streets to disturb the perfect peace we have enjoyed for so long. Very soon we will begin to take statements from you, and I look forward to your cooperation."

Commissioner Coker then turned to his men with orders. "See that these men are given prison clothes before they come dangling their rods at me."

The arrivals, beaten by Commissioner Coker's words, shifted uneasily on the slabs and groaned in pain. They had been cupping their hands to cover their nakedness since their clothes were ripped off them.

Commissioner Coker took one long last look at them and then bounced back to his office. He could be heard talking on the phone. He was inquiring to know whether he was on the line to the chief of security at the

Presidential State House. He then reported he had put every one of his new culprits in custody. The womenfolk were already in their prison, and he was about to take statements from the men.

Grabo hesitated and coughed before summing up courage to beckon to one of the wardens.

"Could you please do me a favor?"

The warden stared at him.

"Eh-eh—could you please check and tell me whether my wife is among the arrested women? And if so, tell her it's me, Grabo, her husband. I heard Mr. Coker saying something about captured women on the phone."

"Call him Commissioner, *Omogbantani!*" the warden shouted with all his breath. Who are you, Mister?"

"Ah—ah—beg pardon—oh," Grabo said. "I shall arrange something for your kindness when I get out of here. She is dressed in—"

However, the warden had no patience to listen to his demands. "Well, Mr. Grabo, or whatever it is you call yourself, don't you worry my friend. If your wife is among the female prisoners, dressed in whatever fashion, we have men here who can take care of her. And I wish you to know that here we are not rewarded for being kind, we are rewarded for being severe."

Grabo twisted his face in anger and spat on the face of the warden. "If you ever touch my wife, I'll kill you. I'll kill you like a dog. I swear to God!"

The other wardens automatically descended on him and dragged him away from the rest. He could be heard cursing and wailing outside. As the wailing faded, the first of the new arrivals was called in to make a statement. Borbor Pain rose from his seat, dressed in a prison uniform, and walked to the door marked Commissioner Dunstant Omotayo Melvin Coker. He was combing his beard with his fingers since he had lost his comb and radio in the raid.

"Whatever you say here will be counted against you in evidence," said Commissioner Coker, looking at the two clerks sandwiching Borbor Pain, ready to write down the statement in red ink. "What is your name?" he bellowed.

In that instant, his door creaked open and in walked a senior officer. He was dying with laughter.

Pointing to Borbor Pain he said, "This is their leader. He is the one referred to as the madman."

Borbor Pain turned and looked at the intruding officer who kept reassuring himself that it was for sure the madman under the cotton tree who told the crowd that the president was about to sell the country. The intruding officer told the commissioner that he had met the man delivering his dangerous speech in front of the cotton tree, making fun of the president, and encouraging the others to take up arms.

"I see, Mr. Madman, that there must have been too much madness in your head," the Commissioner removed his spectacles and took a good look of his prisoner as though all along he had been invisible. Turning to the intruding officer he said, "I guess for lack of a better description of this prisoner we shall write him down as Mr. Madman, and we will make a summary of what that means for his trial."

That was it for Borbor Pain whose name was written down as Mr. Madman. He didn't protest. He just sat there staring at the commissioner. Even when he was asked to begin his statement and even with all the threats the commissioner leveled at him, Borbor Pain did not utter a single word.

It was late at night before the new arrivals were unchained and ushered to their prison cells.

Sore all over after the assault he had endured, Grabo stepped on a soft object that flattened under his foot. He reached down and took it in his finger and smeared it. Bringing it closer for detection he shouted to alert the others and told them he had stepped on excrement. They laughed at him and asked if he didn't smell urine and vomitus in the room as well. Or had he lost his sense of smell after the beating?

Borbor Pain found a corner, sat down, and leaned against the wall. He then reflected on everything that had happened in the day. He thought about his home under the cotton tree and the moist ground which had served as a bed for him. He missed the sea breeze that had always lulled him to sleep. In his new little corner, he felt no comfort, only a tremor. He dozed off.

The narrator suspected that I was slumbering from having stayed awake all night to listen to his long story. He drew in a long breath as if taking into his lungs the long narrative he had so slowly delivered. Just then he disappeared into thin air and I closed my tired eyes.

3

Ten thousand children emerged naked from the dark woods of the peninsula. They ran up the mountain, climbing higher and higher toward the summit. The older ones among them wore calicos around their waists, and the younger ones had shaved their heads to the skin. Barefooted, breathing heavily, they ran up the black animal rock, which five hundred years ago a conquistador, had christened Kaibara, because it reminded him of a land with a hard surface of bad soil and high vexatious mountains.

The children's sweltering bodies merged with the rock. The sun roasted their blood, and their skins dripped with sweat. Another group of ten thousand children, with very much the same appearance, but with guns taller than they were and ammo belts tangled across their chests, chased after the first ten thousand.

Suddenly, I saw myself in the narrow gap between the two groups. The pursued group seized me by the right hand and cried,

"Help us!" The other group, pulling me by the left hand shouted,
"Give way!"
  They began to tear me apart.

The dream soaked me from head to toe.

At once a sore opened in my heart! I couldn't stop sweating. I felt like buckets of tears were running down my face, and the red moon of the devil roaming through my lungs to ignite a pain deep inside me.

My exile was already an old hag dreaming of a coffin full of bones every night. With the new dream, I decided it was time to go home across the threatening seas to my native land and cry over my polychromatic pain.

It was time to come out of exile! My dream prompted a knock, one hundred doors behind me.

In the waking world, I attempted to wade gently through the familiar waters of social intercourse at the height of a hurricane season, trying to reconnect to the world.

A voice told me to begin a journey along the nostalgic route like men of letters. But how was I to begin a letter, for instance, to a woman who had long forgotten me?

How was I to avoid sounding romantic to an old lover when addressing the political affair of the past of my country? Besides, in my exile, the past, the present, and the future had already formed in me something dirty that came from the bowels of the muddy pigs in my forgotten republic.

I remembered reading a book talking about the past being a foreign country. What if, I thought, that past was trapped in the teeth of a hungry alligator?

What if the embers of convoluted events lingered to brighten the mortal cavern of night?

What if the waters of the banked rivers rushed into rude tributaries and washed over the republic so recently reclaimed, precocious although still not fully formed? What if the past was the consequence of a rabid interaction that left the independence emitting unending pus that stank for a while and then dried up?

The thought of a republic writhing like someone raped by a devil bigger than that of any mortal took away all pretext of innocent gentility.

The lugubrious image of Miss Havisham, with her bedraggled wedding dress, stepped out of Charles Dickens' *Great Expectations* and seemed to look out at me from the blank page on which I attempted to set down words to my former mistress, M'balu, who had been renamed Vanessa (a name I had found romantic) by her Krio guardians in the early '50s.

It was fashionable then for natives to be christened with European names. This practice appeared to hang a tag around the necks of black monkeys just rescued from the thick and impenetrable ignorance of the African jungles. European names indicated that their owners had been saved by droplets of water sprinkled on their heads or by having been dipped in the open mouth of bedeviled streams in the full view of a million unfortunate others still buried in the foam of darkness. However, compelled by her traditional roots and the

31

adult shame of her teenage wetness, Vanessa had since reclaimed her native name.

M'balu, my very own Miss Havisham, carried a wound which Victorian England required Dickens to blur in his character. It bled onto the thick layer of dust on her, such as on the wedding dress of colonial promise.

The colonial legacies of makeshift structures and narrow streets in my beloved republic characterized the lugubrious nature of the immediate post-colonial African extracted from a jungle and set to hang on the backdoor of a new civilization continually blown by the harsh wind of European culture.

On the white sheet before me, I wanted to write about the incongruous graffiti of Miss Havisham's dual selves. Each self-seemed to be constantly detaching from the other like two spent dogs in post-coital exhaustion. Each was a shadow of the other, yet appeared very much like an independent entity.

Alienated from my wife and daughter, from both marriage and fatherhood, I experienced the hunger of loneliness. In the beginning, my loneliness flowed through me like a breath of freedom before returning from across mirroring streams smelling of cadaverous stink and coming through the window in skeletal pirate boots to take possession of me in my sleep.

The rest of my life had become a house of windows, vulnerable to the wind of change that sped across New York City at eighty miles per hour. I had never known a word or a phrase, capable of describing this kind of hunger. However, because this hunger brought with it a disturbing physical aspect, like the contractions of a prolonged past, I believed it was real.

In reason, I agreed with my instinct that I must reconnect with my country, Kaibara, if I were ever to know relief from this hunger. With my wife and daughter gone out of my life, I had no friends to hang out with in New York City. Reconnecting with the motherland, therefore, promised nostalgic rejuvenation. Already, vivid African images surged in my head: the noise of an African family cooking the daily meal, the clash of mortar and pestle in the practiced hands of little maids, a crawling man-eating python, and the opportunity of the community man-child to display to the applause of spectators his bravery in wrestling the snake with its vicious teeth.

I still hadn't forgotten the news of the mysterious death of my friend, Archibald in RoMarong City. He had spent his last days in incarceration, living and dying by his conscience. As I considered him, my mind recalled the gleaming beige of the blood-starved republic, but I was soon catapulted into a sense of the present and the future. Thus, I felt the need to be cautious in composing my letter to M'balu.

My dear M'balu, accept my apology for the long silence between us.

I paused to examine what I had written. Something about it seemed inappropriate. To open with an apology I thought might create a psychic tension between M'balu and me, and I didn't want to admit guilt to her for anything I didn't consider wrong on my part. I also convinced myself that with the burden of the war still

heavy on her mind, the sense of presenting myself to
her as a victim might vaguely link me, in her mind, to
Kaibara's butchers, whose spiritual destruction would
undoubtedly remain a deep-seated agony to her.

*My dear M'balu, I always remember you in my prayers. God
knows that a fine person like you has no reason to be locked up in
the mess our country has been thrown into.*

I felt uneasy about what I had written, but I lacked the
will to work on my wording. The ineluctable power of
the words reverberated in me. I was impressed that the
words sharply and directly expressed my feelings for
both Kaibara and M'balu. Though I was not so sure
that God knew M'balu anymore as a fine person, I was
equally unsure if some wicked god had thrown Kaibara
into the war that now devastated it.

I felt that M'balu should have repudiated the choice of
her parents just as I felt that Kaibara should have
known better than to haul itself into the mess into
which it was now sinking.

In writing a letter to an estranged but long-standing
acquaintance such as M'balu, I would do well to recall
some of the striking moments we had spent together.
Looking up from the paper, I let my gaze fall upon the
Venetian blinds in front of me where M'balu was fading
in as a newly lighted candle. As I stared at them, I saw
in my mind the washed garment dragged from under
bodies in a battlefield, imprinted with the many images
of *my* Miss Havisham as she turned from an aborted
wedding. Pale white hung as though dripping the blood
of ten thousand wars.

M'balu quickly vanished behind the Venetian slats into unseen moments. I persuaded myself to believe that if I lifted those blinds and allowed my perception a free rein, I would not only wash my mind of battlements, but also I would regain a handful of memorable events of our past together.

Walking toward the window, I recited her name. I must have said it ten times before reaching the blinds. "M'balu" conveyed granite warmth whereas the "Vanessa" counterpart simply mesmerized. However, for the sake of the letter I set myself to write, I needed to stay hard and dry.

Beyond my window, New York City's river flowed before me like the sagacious RoMarong City River on the edge of my beloved Kaibara. The RoMarong City River ran into the Atlantic Ocean where the Creek broke its neck and spread below the city, giving rise to my Nova Scotian, dark Anglo-Saxon Krio ancestry.

At once I heard the rolling of the parched waves and imagined them exploding against the pubescent legs of M'balu. She was there, surrendering her body to the golden sand upon which she curled in serpentine bliss, her hands held high above the water in the salubrious wind, beckoning me to join her in defying the *munkle,* a Themne word she had taught me. It jumped into my head, liberated from its attendant meaning. Yet as I fabricated a role for *munkle,* I heard M'balu whispering to me from the alcoves of a raw feminine independence that *munkle* stood for the sea waves. At that moment, the brilliant color of one memorable moment rushed to mind.

"It's not fair, Desmond! It's not fair!" M'balu had shouted to me across Lumley Beach that diluted the impassioned brutality of the waves.

I shouted back without raising my head, "Almost finished, darling. The paper is almost through writing itself!"

"How can you do that to me? Did I come here to watch you bow over political papers? You are spoiling the fun. Even the sea takes notice of your quaint behavior! Must I—"

"Almost there, darling," I insisted. "At the tail end of it, the very tail end," I paused for a moment and closed the gap between us. "I'm sure you want to see me make a good impression tomorrow, don't you?" I asked.

She stood before me like a serpent, her nudity inspiring a liquid attraction. My eyes followed the water rivulets that trickled down her thighs. Lost in her legend, I failed to realize she had seized the papers I was working on and neatly tossed them inside one of the bags. Then she dove headlong into the water, beckoning me to follow. When she broke the surface she discovered me standing and mapping out her body's complex shape. We both plunged, she in my arms and me wrapped between her legs.

We resurfaced and achieved a watery balance.

"You mean so much to me," I said.

She understood what I meant.

Her stare came upon me as bright as oil on Harmattan skin. I inhaled its fire.

"Why then wouldn't you allow yourself to mean the same to me at this moment? My time with you is limited. Soon you'll be shackled by the watchful eyes of your Krio girl," she said, placing her palms against the surface of the water as she hung her head.

I quickly realized how hard it was for her to open her heart. I wanted to tease her. How well she had practiced her speech considering how reserved she had always been about letting me into her mind. I knew that this was her moment, and the best I could do was not to discourage her while her eyes poured *marro* (as she called oil in her language).

I thrust a leg between hers and with one hand pulled her toward me, allowing for the water to lap between us. Making love in the middle of a torrent was not something I dared, but I pulled off a clever stunt. I allowed the gushing water to overturn me. I brought my head to brush against her hair as we let the jealous waves wash us ashore.

"I know I have to watch you speak tomorrow at the rally, but I'll not be as close to you as I'm right now or as I would like to be then. Allow me the pleasure of recalling this moment while you growl into that microphone of yours." M'balu had barely finished her words when she dragged me again into the water, both of us laughing at the exuberant earnestness of her words.

That was in the late 1960s, a long time ago. Kaibara had just begun realizing the promise of its independence. The British had gone, but they hadn't turned their backs on us. I had then just returned from Britain where I had studied law when I walked into the house of my conservative parents, who were already armed with my future wife, as they had insisted my life partner must not come from the natives but from the maroon Nova Scotian settlers whose lineage I had born into.

They had been categorically insistent on M'balu's dismissal.

At that time, the maniacal steps of my country's burgeoning independence scared my Krio tribesmen. Politics had already slipped from their grasp, but they had continued to consider themselves uncanny nation-builders and the vanguard of civilization with their higher education and their fine European manners. They were prepared to guard the last remnant of their monomaniac position by any means necessary.

My parents admired my wife's upbringing and her colorful training at a respected 18th century institution for girls named after a British teenager who knew nothing about Kaibara, but before they even could acquaint me with the information about her, I had fallen in deep with M'balu.

Returning to the present and armed with the sweet memory of the beach, I dashed back to the table and grabbed the pen.

I can still picture your smile and your November image spread across the golden sand of Lumley Beach. It pains me to imagine that the sad events taking place in our country today may have dimmed those sharp eyes of yours that were a mirror into mine. Your surging image carried by your sculpted legs pounces on my

imagination. I can still hear your gait on the carpet grass of my
parents' compound as you defied their discrimination and threats
to cup a kiss from my mouth; dressed to your taste, my simple
M'balu of a humble countrified background. ...

I paused in stupefaction, recognizing that again I was
going astray by beginning to list the romantic at the
expense of the informational. Would a former mistress
currently "embroiled in a war," to borrow a phrase
from my estranged wife, be interested in reading my
romantic letter? Would the evil angel not have strewn
ill luck for M'balu along her path of survival and
security in this time of war? No matter, I was already
brimming with memories of a woman I hadn't seen in
over thirty years.

I continued despite my misgivings.

I must confess I don't know the true nature of the war in
Kaibara. I'm disturbed by descriptions of the conflict. Many of
my American friends, who themselves have seen the wars in
Vietnam and Korea, label our war in Kaibara a mere civil matter
that doesn't necessarily qualify as a war. They say that it entails
mostly a civil disturbance meant to render the country
ungovernable and that the organizers only wish for the government
to listen to them. I wonder how your father, being a Burma
veteran, would have described it.

I have also seen such phrases as, "senseless war in Kaibara,"
printed in American newspapers. I'm totally baffled by this
description! I believe anyone who has followed the political history
of Kaibara would never call the conflict senseless. What is your
experience in this matter?

I understand the death toll has risen beyond previous records. It
is also sad to hear that the war has tribal undertones. Is this

39

true? M'balu, I'm grateful you and I never knew this antagonism in our youth. I realize my parents preferred for me a Krio wife to you, a Themne girl. Oh, oh why am I bringing this up again? But it was just like your parents preferred for you a native husband to me; nevertheless, you and I never harbored hostilities. Consider for instance the Fitzjohns, distant relatives of mine, who saw to it that you had a good education at a training college, how they brought you up like their own kid. Your parents were perfectly willing to give you over to them when you were five, as you yourself told me, sweet Vanessa.

I hesitated again, fearing I had become too general in my letter. Then I thought that after such a lengthy estrangement from a former mistress, a reconnecting letter to her ought to be intensely personal.

Outside my apartment, a noiseless rain fell as the dust of evening crept in. Streetlights glowed brighter and brighter against the deepening dark; a caustic wind flailed against and around the indifferent buildings of New York City. Every thirty minutes two or three airplanes combed the edges of the sky, and life in the streets and on the sidewalks proceeded with scientific locomotion.

I took a glass from the cabinet over the sink and from the cupboard shelf pulled a bottle of bubonic red wine and a lime. Moments later, I was sipping to my heart's relief. I tried to think about my wife's action, searching for any reasonable excuse that had sent her packing with our daughter, Yolanda. It was already a year and a half since they left, and she had continued to talk to me through our daughter. Whenever Yolanda visited, the phrase, "a country in the middle of a war," managed to come up.

"You don't have to remind me that my country is in the middle of a war? You only know Kaibara from what you hear. Why do you insist on saying inappropriate phrases?" That was typical of my response.

"But Kaibara is at war, Daddy, and there is no way you can walk right into the middle of affairs to 'change' things."

I knew my daughter was defensive as always. I had long ago agreed that Yolanda was right, and she knew how to put words in tonal quotation marks to appeal to my psyche. I also felt that those very words were a heavy backhand slap at me, feeding me all that crap of being patriotic. It was that last feeling that filled me with a deep rage.

"Is it not enough though that I'm not in any state of war!" I would say with a noisy arrogance. "My mind is free and the inside of me has already reopened all the doors of yesterday. I will do what I want! Your mother will not shout me down, not even with your help."

Yolanda never wanted her mother to creep into our conversations. It always brought a fire of silence from her, but she always remained calm. It occurred to me we were both pulling a rope, straining at opposite ends, watching for the red ribbon tied around its center, each of us hoping to see it closer, to be the first person to shout, "Hurrah!" Yolanda, however, only looked into the glass of wine, if she was drinking, with a casual frustration over an image that kept eluding her; never ready to give that shout.

41

"Why do you have to remind me about the war in my country?" I insisted in asking the question with the aim of cutting into her torment with a soothing balm of words.

"Technically, it is also my country, Dad," Yolanda muttered.

One night, I cried like a baby while pouring her a second glass of wine. It was one of those times when she had not seen me for days. Then that night, on her way to a job with a local charity, she breezed in. She met me drinking the wine she had presented me on my birthday. As usual, I had many questions for her, but she let them pass unanswered. It was typical of her to ignore my questions if she felt like it. In doing so, she would raise her chin higher than usual when sipping her wine and shut her eyes, disappearing for a brief spell into a world of her own.

Seeing her like that disturbed me more and more. Over time my questions to her sounded more like statements than inquiries. I never repeated them. Later we talked about the things she preferred to talk about. However, when I began wanting answers from her, she would sigh heavily and stare straight ahead. At this point, after she returned from her state of "*herself-ness*," she routinely opted for lighter and noncommittal conversations. I had always respected her emotions, considering that her mother's separation from me had already traumatized her.

We often talked about the adults whom I taught at the literacy center. That kind of topic interested Yolanda. She loved to hear about my experiences and about my

42

new past time. I loved to tell her how back home the average Kaibaran never believed that there were white people, for that matter Americans, who didn't know how to read and write. That subject or any other topic was fine, but she would not allow me to discuss her mother beyond my usual inquiries of her health.

I loved Yolanda's questions about Kaibara, no matter how silly they were. On many occasions when she visited me directly from the library, she brought printed pages of African news from the Internet. I was proud that she was taking full advantage of the American dream and at twenty-four was completing graduate school. I had encouraged her to follow in my profession, but she had shown little aptitude for law, opting instead for child psychology. I thought it quaint and an ill match to her spiritual mindset, but I never said so. She had also developed an interest in writing poetry, which she preferred to call verses. When she was nineteen, she wrote several of them she wanted me to read for her. Later some of them appeared in her college literary journal; others (sadly, those I found wonderful) she condemned, shredded, and fed to the wastebasket.

"Oh, Daddy, they are not good pieces," she would say.

Yolanda didn't talk much about boys. Once when I tried to initiate a discussion on the subject, she simply waved her left hand and told me that the topic sucked. I insisted it was an important subject since at her age temptations weren't to be ruled out. Although I pressed her, believing she was merely being reserved, I remained aware of a father's limits in such matters. So, throwing my hands in the air, I remarked that I had given up, but not without adding, at least for my own satisfaction, that I hoped her mother and she discussed such issues.

"Of course we do, Dad. I'm glad you know that it's a women's issue."

With a broad smile, she promptly terminated the topic. Then, reaching for her glass of wine, she gulped it down and left, as usual, unceremoniously.

I let the letter sit on the table for two days before returning to it. In that time it was as if the phrases had adapted their meanings to suit my desire although nothing about them had changed. The anomalies that earlier abraded me had vanished. The letter now sounded as real to me as M'balu had become in my dreams.

The devil of memory has a way of lingering once invoked.

Again I picked up the pen and began to write.

Allow me to inquire about your family members. Would it be awful of me to ask whether anyone among them has died in the war? I'm sorry that I'm only now getting in touch with you. The truth is I haven't had any contact information for you.

You understand the circumstances under which I left RoMarong City. There was scarcely time for me to send you a note to say I was leaving. Archibald was in prison when I left, and my parents had gone into hiding. The pain of seeing my face plastered in the Daily Mail *along with pleas for information leading to my arrest nearly killed me.*

The picture of you I carried in my wallet was a source of constant comfort. At every opportunity, I gazed at it and even spoke to it in words I cannot now remember. However, I remember sharing it with the American Ambassador before I ventured out of his embassy building that ugly October night with heavy thunder roaring overhead. I had been hiding there for three days and nights. As I groped my way through the dark, I carried with me your picture—no, it had in fact become your real image to me by then—shielded from the angry rain by my dirty suit.

I never imagined for a moment that three decades would pass, and still we haven't seen each other! I cannot help thinking that the rebellion came much too late. It pains me to think that there are people with no substance and with no moral ties to our country who hijacked it and so tainted its splendid history! I have heard many stories about the war and the various interests underlying it, but the irresponsible response by the government targeting innocent civilians and the display of their faces in international papers, as sober government officials continue to torment and frustrate me.

However, my hope is sustained by the resilience of Borbor Pain. I know him as a man who had given all his life to fighting against the dictatorship of the first president of Kaibara, a man whom I served. I am sure you are aware that it was his second military coup that he and others had staged that had led to my exile after it was foiled. I do not want to go deeply into that matter in this letter for I do not know into whose hands my letter would fall. But I am sure you still recollect that the coup had happened after the government was going to introduce a one party state to try to keep the president in power for ever. I had opposed that unpatriotic plan. So after the coup had failed, as an insider who was accused of having betrayed the cause, I became a target of the government. Never did I imagine that my opposition to the

45

government for our Kaibara would mean I would never see you again.

I felt lighter with each sentence. The letter grew into a cathartic event, the tone of which was carried and shaped by the scores of internal conversations I'd held onto, conversations my wife and daughter had denied me in the years of our separation. Rising to the surface of the letter was the hunger I'd had to endure through countless arid moments when my wife and my daughter had shut me out of their world.

I wrote of many other things. I had by now taken full control of the good times M'balu and I spent together. I reminded her of her college graduation ceremony, the evening ball, and my urgent attempt at persuading her to spend that night at my place for the very first time.

The letter consumed three sheets. I read it repeatedly, each time finding something to add or rephrase. The more I read it, the more I realized what had been left unsaid. For creating an effect and arousing her interest, I shifted some of the paragraphs. However, with larger events of our past looming in my mind, it became clear that what I retained in memory would always remain superior to what I could ever hope to say in writing.

Reluctantly I signed it, *Desmond Johnson.*

I reexamined the characters on the page. Each meaning-filled word was overwhelming, each detail overflowing with unspoken reminders of our romance. Suddenly, my heart missed a beat! How ungrateful M'balu would think of me after so many years to write as if we had merely shared a casual night in Lumley Beach.

Cut by the blades of guilt, I tore the letter to bits, rolled the fragments into little balls, and threw them into the trashcan. I collected and set before me more blank sheets of papers, laid my pen across the pile, and descended into thought. This was in the year 1996 and the cool autumn wind of New York rudely collided against my windows.

4

The narrator took me to the highest point of a mountain I didn't know. He said to me that the longer the story the higher the narrator and the audience needed to be elevated. He sat me on a pillar of cloud and told me to refrain from looking below. In fear I looked into his intense eyes and a strong confidence returned to me. He continued from where he had stopped the last time:

The distant crashing of doors rudely interrupted the sleeping Borbor Pain. Around him in the dark the other prisoners were snoring amidst the excrement and urine left behind by paroled inmates.

Prior to falling asleep Borbor Pain had felt sorry for his cellmates who were protesting the stench they had been locked into. Now they were all sleeping like the dead, breathing the stench into their lungs and their lives.

One thing even Commissioner Coker didn't know was that Dembapa Prison wasn't a strange place to Borbor Pain. His last lockup had been for shooting a minister who was delivering a public address at a government function. The camera he had used was immediately confiscated. Three policemen arrested him for unauthorized snapshots and whisked him to Dembapa Prison where he was abandoned without charge. One day a warden mistook him for an idler and urged him away before the commissioner in his fury locked him up.

The growing noise outside of the cell startled Borbor Pain to his feet. He cautiously picked his way in the dark to reach the door. He stretched himself and saw a dim light on the other side. He heard footsteps in the corridor and the thunderous crashing of doors.

The thick darkness gave him no clue what hour it was. He could hear frogs croaking, their noses buried in mud. As if the frogs weren't enough, thousands of mosquitoes whined in the cell, protesting the approaching roar. The sound of tumbling objects accompanied the rambunctious noise.

"What's going on here?" A voice out of the dark asked.

Borbor Pain nearly sprang from the door when he heard the voice. It was Grabo. He too had crouched on his legs, on the heavy weight of his sores to reach the door. Borbor Pain stood still for a while to calm his accelerated heartbeat.

"I don't know yet, I was trying to find out when you scared me," he said.

The noise increased in volume as indistinct voices grew louder in the dark corridor. The footsteps too sounded louder like accompanying drumbeats.

"This sounds like some jubilation," said Borbor Pain. "Listen."

"Happiness in this hell? I bet it's the commissioner's men whipping some inmates," Grabo countered.

Borbor Pain turned to examine his partner. He was able to see Grabo's round face in the dim light. "Do you know how long I've been coming in here?" he asked.

Grabo gave him a sharp look. "Have you been here before? You, a madman?"

"You may say so. I'm experienced enough to recognize every noise I hear within these walls," he ran his fingers through his beard and thought of his comb.

"Have you been here before?" Grabo asked again.

Borbor Pain nodded.

"Wait a minute. Aren't you a madman? How could they have brought you in here?"

"That's what you all say," Borbor Pain answered smiling. "But I tell you what, we all are mad under this system. Hardship is the forerunner of madness. Or is it the other way around?"

"Eh...eh...eh...you—listen to me," Grabo spoke harshly. "You are a troublesome person. I don't know why you're doing this, but I'm a happily married man who hates to put the life of my family at risk."

"The point is we are all at risk whether someone puts us at it or not," Borbor Pain said.

Reaching for Grabo's hand, Borbor Pain squeezed it hard and whispered to him, "Keep quiet, I think they are here! I hear them closer. This is no time for distraction."

Almost at once two men emerged as if they came from under them. Grabo wondered whether they had been listening to their conversation. The men carried pickaxes in their hands, and on their backs hung AK47 rifles. They were in military fatigues, their hands covered in black mackintosh gloves.

Apparently they had been forging the way ahead of the rowdy crowd. Wherever they went, there was a door, and wherever there was a door, they crashed it open. As the two men prepared to strike the door to Grabo and Borbor Pain's cell, they noticed the two prisoners. They hesitated before they thunderously commanded them to withdraw from it.

"You're about to be free men!" one of them said. "If you'll just move a little back and protect your faces, this door is coming down in a moment."

Borbor Pain and Grabo drew a considerable distance back from the door and eagerly awaited their freedom. The two strange men hit the door twice on the hinges and it went tumbling down.

"How many of you are in here? Listen, you must not attempt to go your own ways. There is a crowd coming behind us. Make sure you join it and follow us. We're all going to leave here in one piece. If you attempt to go out separately, we're not responsible for the outcome, and we'll do nothing to help you. Instead we'll probably kill you if you try to wander off and endanger the rest of the group."

The two men disappeared from sight like the wind. Their pickaxes could be heard crashing on other cell doors ahead in the corridor. An uproarious crowd was fast approaching. The other inmates were now up from their sleep and were anxious to know what was happening. The cell became brighter as the crowd approached. Many carried torches and candles in their hands with additional ones to distribute.

The collective crowd marched into the open compound. There stood a group of men fully dressed as if they had been on the battlefield. Some more were scattered about in civilian clothing singing revolutionary songs. Occasionally, slogans like, 'Liberate the Motherland!' 'Slavery lasted for years, but Freedom lasts forever!' and 'Make me a poor man but give me my freedom in my motherland!' came the shrill voices of the women, their words swallowed by the urgency of the event.

Examining the scene further, Borbor Pain noticed a number of prison wardens handcuffed and roped to old train rails leaning against the administrative buildings. Those wardens who had resisted lay sprawled dead on the ground. As he was taking in the scene, a soldier approached Borbor Pain and handed him a gun.

"You are one of us, I presume."

Before Borbor Pain could respond, the soldier continued. "Handle this gun carefully and stay here, old man. I must go and drink some water."

The soldier was gone before Borbor Pain could properly make him out.

Two men walked to the center of the crowd and began calling everyone to order.

The night was slowly moving into the early hours of morning. Darkness still hung in the air and a cool breeze fanned the crowd. The metal gates leading into the prisons were lying on the ground as though they had always been down like that. Many other prisoners ran in and out of the administrative building with loot they had taken from the wardens' quarters.

When the two men in the center of the crowd gave the command for the group to keep moving, a woman aimed a rifle at the sky and blasted a shot off. Scared, Borbor Pain looked keenly at the gun in his hand and wondered whether he was to drop it or use it.

Where was the owner?

Well, he couldn't wait for him any longer, the command had been given. The gun was no stranger in his hands. If he must move with the crowd with a gun in his hands, he must move like a soldier.

Suddenly gunshots ricocheted outside the prison compound. The shots came in rapid succession. It was easy to tell they were coming from superior machines. Brilliant fire ran through the blackness of the night. Frogs with their noses buried in mud went silent. The wind swept noiselessly through the compound. Everything stood still to listen to the gunshots.

A well-dressed man, worn out by the night's activities threw his hands in the sky as he pleaded for attention. A few men around him supported him.

"My name is Raster, but there seems to be no time here to make speeches. We are all going to try to get out of this prison alive."

The guns still blasted outside the prison compound.

"For our own safety we have to stick together and fight together. Nobody must show any sign of fear, the situation is under control," he disappeared into the crowd.

"Right now we have been attacked," said a soldier. "Let's get out of here and defend ourselves!" Following his directions, the crowd hurried toward the fallen gates. Rifles soon became available for everyone. Grabo grabbed one and looked about, fearful. His eyes met those of Borbor Pain.

"Every man for himself! God for us all!" Borbor Pain shouted to him.

Grabo wanted to ask him what this was all about, but the fire he saw in the eyes of his partner silenced him.

The shots were now too close for comfort. Bullets were flying into the compound like hailstones. Borbor Pain cocked his gun and took aim at the invisible attackers and released five bullets. Grabo admired him and confessed that for his own part, he had never carried a gun before. However, there was hardly any time for lectures, so Borbor Pain told Grabo to emulate him.

The group had left them behind and headed for the gate.

Suddenly Grabo alerted Borbor Pain that the officer who had removed their shoes was approaching.

A chill ran through Grabo's body as Borbor Pain cocked his gun again.

"Don't shoot," shouted the officer. "All right, don't you shoot! We are together in this. I'm one of you."

Disregarding him, Borbor Pain took aim. Before he released the trigger, a man who stood nearby quickly confirmed the officer's claim. Borbor Pain dropped his hands to his sides.

"Well, will you explain to us what this freedom is all about?" Grabo said.

"We will come to that, gentlemen, but for now here is what I have for you," the warden threw a plastic bag to the ground in front of them. "You can have your shoes back. You are not going to walk out of those gates barefoot," he smiled. "You are sure better than all the lords and great men I have served in this prison."

The two men reached for their shoes and put them on.

"You want to kill?" the officer asked. "We still have the enemies behind us."

"Ah, yes, I guess it's time for Grabo to practice," Borbor Pain said.

"You mean I kill them?" Grabo asked.

"No, you shoot them," Borbor Pain said.

"But they'll die!" said Grabo, trembling.

"Then they die. They wanted you dead, remember? These men lack the conscience of the ant. Treat them the way they treat others."

Neither Grabo nor the officer knew what Borbor Pain meant. They thought it was one of his moods of madness.

Down by the fallen gate the battle was tense. Sporadic gunshots erupted between the escaping prisoners and the repelling force. The attackers were also using mortar bombs and RPGs. Outside the prisons, two or three houses were already on fire. Within the compound a few people were screaming. Many corpses lay on the ground.

Borbor Pain spotted Commissioner Coker busy pleading for mercy to a drunken soldier who kept playfully aiming his gun at the man's chest. Borbor Pain moved slowly toward him and then jumped, causing Commissioner Coker to scream. He enquired about the commissioner's staff, but when the commissioner hesitated, Borbor Pain shot his left hand at close range. Then he grabbed his victim's hand, dipped into his oozing blood and licked it.

"I like this water," he said.

"That's my blood, you madman!" the commissioner cried.

Borbor Pain's expression changed. His eyes blinked and grew intense. In one stroke of anger he aimed for the commissioner's forehead and pulled the trigger.

"This is for writing me down in ink as being mad!"

It would be a few years later before the civil war broke out. However, in the instant, and just having been rescued from prison, and far into the forests of Jepehun, two hundred miles away and twelve hours of bad roads on truck from RoMarong City, Borbor Pain and Grabo could still not tell what was happening around them. They had left behind tens of corpses as they escaped from the city with the crowd. A piece of shrapnel had entered Grabo and ripped his right leg so badly that he had to be carried on the back of Borbor Pain. Grabo was in bad spirits and had demanded to know what was going on when they hit the outskirts of RoMarong City. He had told Borbor Pain he planned on defecting from what he called this violent group, explaining that he thought their saviors were nothing other than criminals who had come to kidnap them for some wild ransom.

The guns were silent. The road was long, and the crowd was urged to hurry for the start of the journey that was on foot. In the quiet of the still night a shot was fired at the back of the group. What was it? The prisoners stopped. A soldier ran to the front and explained to his colleagues that a man had tried to defect so he had shot him dead.

Just like that? Grabo couldn't believe his ears. What then was the freedom in the deal? Why were the ringleaders not telling them what was going on? The crowd continued to move on. Were they all going to be killed in the woods? They were on the road until daylight of the next day. In the forest woods of Jepehun, they caught up with a larger crowd of people. At the intersection of a small river, two leaders, one from each band, walked up to each other and embraced. The leader from Borbor Pain's crowd had introduced himself as Raster. Soon after the meeting between the leaders, the two crowds spilled over and became one.

Borbor Pain didn't believe his eyes. In the crowd joining his group were many great men and women, all attired in formal dress, as though they were attending a state function. Then he caught sight of two white and two Arab men. A flag was being mounted, but it was not the Kaibara flag. Instead three strange colors were flying above his head.

On the far end of the forest, five soldiers beckoned to the rest of the crowd to go to the side. These series of events made no sense to Grabo who was in great pain. He looked at Borbor Pain and told him so. He started to say something more when a soldier walked up to him and sternly asked him what his problem was.

"It's my leg. It's paining me," Grabo said.

"What? Were you shot?" the soldier asked.

"No, I stepped on a shrapnel."

"Why do you stand here grinning and grumbling to yourself? Why don't you go over to the mobile clinic over there and get your leg treated?"

Grabo didn't believe his ears. Could these men who wanted to kill everyone provide healing for the wounded? Continuing to stare at the soldier, Grabo dragged himself in the direction the soldier had pointed. Suddenly he remembered that he was going to ask Borbor Pain what his real name was apart from being referred to as the mad man when the soldier interrupted. Since he still didn't know it, he didn't know how to address him. He wanted Borbor Pain to know that he would be rejoining him soon.

"Go get you registered, old man," the soldier said, tapping Borbor Pain on the shoulder. Borbor Pain shrugged as though he had been awakened from a deep sleep.

He joined the long, slow-moving line of registrants. Looking far ahead, he saw the two men who had embraced each other in the company of the white and Arab men. They were exchanging cigarettes and lighters. Laughter erupted from among them. Two white women majestically walked up to join their group. They held cigarettes between their fingers, and one of them carried a briefcase in her other hand. After a few moments, she handed the briefcase over to one of the white men.

Borbor Pain's mind raced back to RoMarong City and all that had happened in what seemed like a minute to him. He recalled the bullet he had lodged in the skull of Commissioner Coker. He had not waited to see him die. Why had he really killed the commissioner? Given a second opportunity to face a live Commissioner Coker again, he would surely pull the trigger on him again. He had disgust for the commissioner for officially writing him down as being a madman.

He suddenly felt like vomiting when he recalled how he had licked the commissioner's blood. He knew it was not really him who had tasted the blood. It was— but that was the strange thing about his visions. Whenever he wanted them to be real they appeared to him as illusions and came real when he wished they were illusions.

"And you, what's your name and occupation?" the lecherous registrar thundered in the ear of Borbor Pain in order to return him from the loggia of his lost world.

Scared and turning to look at the registrar, Borbor Pain gave his name in full, adding that he was a retired soldier of the Kaibara Army and a former photographer on the side. He saluted and stood at alert, still thinking about the Dembapa Road escape, which had taken twelve hours before they could finally arrive in Jepehun.

5

Borbor Pain, also known as the mad man, knew how much effort he had used his whole life to stay on top of events that interested him. However, it would seem he always kept up with the wrong events at the wrong place and the wrong time. Perhaps at the wrong place and at the wrong time, okay, but on the wrong events, he wouldn't agree. Consequently he had suffered one agony too many, resulting in the loss of many a promising social standing. He had wondered if human beings were astrologically endowed and their stars destined to shine to specific brilliance. Nevertheless, for a man who carried every scar of his destiny on him, he had kept hoping that someday accidental angels could betray their oaths and make available to him matters exclusively meant for gods.

He believed very much in predictions not being destinies but hurdles to overcome in order to achieve one's goals.

His birth had cost his mother her life. He had been born with a shell in his right ear, and a shaken birth attendant had almost declared him a stillbirth. It was later predicted he would be an anarchist, exerting devastating effort toward saving a situation, but no one had ever disclosed this information to him. Even if anyone had, he would hardly have been stopped by such esoteric sentimentalities.

Borbor Pain's intelligence possessed him like deep-rooted anger. It gave him a great deal of charm and occasionally sent him into fits of rage. The mild outbursts came into his head as visions.

He had very little patience with structural learning and hated educators since the day he took his first examination in the presence of strange supervisors. On his own, he had read voraciously and chased after knowledge in his own way. Borbor Pain knew that he needed knowledge for smartness, and that once he was smart, he would himself become knowledge.

He read Plato in one sitting and realized he wanted to become a philosopher-king. Shaka Zulu, Napoleon, and Hitler were great men to him. He adored and worshipped them. As a young man, he had embraced the glamour of political independence in his country when it was served on a silver platter. Listening to the post-independent speech of the first post-colonial Kaibaran leader, he knew at once that power was destined to be a republican prey.

Borbor Pain had dropped out of high school and had briefly chased after the wind. When he came to his senses, he signed up for the military. He remained a corporal until he was discharged for what the records called "subversive and rebellious" behavior while over the years the least among his squad mates had risen to the rank of colonel in the army.

When he was a soldier, Borbor Pain had nurtured a big ambition, a certain kind of people stood in his way. He hated politicians and thought that his happiest moments would be when he had an opportunity to slay them all, put his feet in their shoes, and flood his country's streets with milk and honey.

Shortly after independence, Borbor Pain co-organized the first and second military coups in Kaibara in a bid to seize political power. On each attempt, he had been caught, tried, and jailed. After the second attempt, he was dishonorably discharged from the army and forced to become a photographer in remote areas of his country in order to eke out a living. Years later, his co-plotters found their way into mainstream politics and rose to positions of standing. He didn't know why he had begun to compensate himself by shooting them with his camera at public functions.

Whenever he measured his life against the successes of his childhood friends and squad mates in the army, he developed a protean anger within a paranoiac passion. At thirty, he thought he would rule the world. Having failed at that, he decided to punish his body and his soul. It occurred to him that the only way to do so was to declare himself a vagabond and a self-exile, and to cover his face with a silver beard. Over the years, no one had recognized him.

Borbor Pain stood still, familiarizing himself with the forests of Jepehun. He, like many others, was still wearing his prison uniforms. They fit him as though the tailor had taken his measurement and sewn them in one sitting. He carried himself about the forests with the full awareness that he still remained a prisoner, only transferred from government custody to what looked to him like a gang trap. However, he was by now aware that with the presence of men he knew to be respected statesmen and the presence of white men, women, and Arab men, something noble was being hatched under those huge sheltering trees.

Close to him was Grabo who had returned from the mobile clinic with his leg wound properly treated and bandaged and his name registered in the book. Borbor Pain saw a bright smile returning to the face of his partner who had, since he was injured, remained bitter. Even in the worst circumstances, the assuaging of pain could hold problems at bay for at least a while. Grabo was gazing about at the encampment and the woods beyond. He wondered whether the explanation for this yet unexplained situation in Jepehun following the dramatic breaking of his cell door and the exodus from Dembapa Prisons lay in the dark and foreboding woods.

It seemed to Grabo that the number of people in the forest increased every moment. Soon the entire encampment was filled with people shifting about to accommodate each other and the new arrivals. Grabo hinted to Borbor Pain that everyone appeared to be free and unsupervised. However, the corporal had advised Grabo to use a more longsighted vision. Grabo froze when his eyes beheld dark shadows with extra M16s on their backs and crouched in the distant forests. Each figure carried a number of ammo belts across his chest.

Suddenly a voice blared from a loudspeaker. "Testing the mike," said the voice.

The phrase was repeated about six times before the mike went dead, but the crowd sat riveted. The two men who had embraced each other earlier continued to busy themselves with some organizing. The white and Arab men still continued to talk among themselves under a shady tree as though they were not part of all the activities going on in the camp.

Grabo and Borbor Pain drifted over to a rock and sat down, settling into a deep silence. They could hear murmurs and bits of conversations from the crowd. Grabo felt as though he and his new companion were spectators watching a soccer match. They were far removed from the maddening crowd.

"Grabo I'm truly sorry for your wife," Borbor Pain said.

He noticed Grabo didn't shift his eyes from the woods. Instead he only heaved a big sigh. "I understand how you feel. I felt your pain the moment I heard you asking about your wife at the Dembapa Prison. I'm truly sorry."

"Nyakoi. She is Nyakoi. We have three lovely kids. I have never known another woman since meeting her. I have always given her a sense of security around me. I spoiled her with much caring. I worked hard to provide for her. She is true and faithful to me. I remember telling her the day of our incarceration that I live only for her and the kids."

He bowed his head. He was a man quick to tears. His mother once told him he carried too much of a woman in him. He had proved his mother right when he mourned his father's death for three days on the office steps of a medical doctor who said he would not touch the old man unless the money to secure the required equipment was available. At first, when everyone was crying and blaming the doctor, it was Grabo who had seen reason and explained to his mother that the doctor was not being wicked. "If the doctor begins any operation without the required tools, Papa will die."

The doctor, only beginning his practice, had also told Grabo that he was not prepared to lose customers over Grabo's father, but neither Grabo nor any of the angry relatives had the money to pay. Grabo had actually cried not only for his father but also for the poverty that had plagued his family since he was born into it.

Grabo himself had struggled hard to raise a family of his own, a dream he had while apprenticing at the store of a Lebanese merchant. Grabo's honesty and hard work had won him the heart of the Lebanese merchant. For eight years Grabo slaved under the Lebanese merchant, from selling wares at his store to caring for the merchant's father who needed assisted living.

If Grabo knew that the merchant was underpaying him, he did not say so. He learned to shape his wants according to his wages. Being a single man then, he found it very easy to adjust. His mother had died the year he began to work, and he'd had to rely on the good will of his new master to afford a burial for her. Grabo wanted to live a happy life so he took a wife only when he knew he could maintain one, and for nine years he cared for her as was expected of any husband.

When the birth of his first child approached, Grabo told his boss that he wanted to leave him, adding that he was prepared to work a six-month period without pay if his boss would be kind enough to supply him with wares that he could retail. Grabo would pay for the ware at the end of every month. Within two years, Grabo had become an important name in the association for petty traders in the city.

"If I should die in this bush, I will leave behind me three children who shall die in the same way my father died," Grabo wailed to Borbor Pain.

"You need a positive mind to get out of this, Grabo. We all do, "Borbor Pain told his new friend.

"When I think of it, I hate myself for standing there listening to you saying all that stuff about the president. I guess we didn't think you were a dangerous man. Everyone thought you were mad," Grabo confessed. "We convinced ourselves that the government wouldn't take you seriously."

Borbor Pain shut his eyes and felt one of his visions returning, but he shook himself hard to ward it off. This was a bad moment to lose hold of reality. What if the crowd was asked to move on? He would be sitting there lost in his vision like a man seized by fit.

"I think you were right though," Grabo said. "You exhibited a keen insight into what is currently happening in our country. The trouble, I think, is that you know too much. And hearing what you were saying under that cotton tree, people would think that you were calling for an uprising."

"You know I think it all has to do with the visions I get," Borbor Pain said.

"Visions?"

"Yes, visions. I see things," Borbor Pain explained. "Only they are sometimes not clear to me. One thing I do know is that what I have gone through has made me strong. It's like there is something inside me doing the things I do. It's funny, this thing inside me does not control me, but once it wants something done, I'm willing to do it. I'm always aware that I agree to do what I'm told. I have the will to deny, but I don't have the power or the desire to ignore it. I can tell you that although I killed the warden I *really* didn't kill him."

Grabo gave Borbor Pain a sympathetic look. In his day-to-day life in RoMarong City, he would never have believed that he would one day sit with Borbor Pain to discuss issues of the heart. If he considered the ordeal he had gone through a dream—a bad dream—it was because he had kept telling himself Borbor Pain was a big joke.

"Corporal!" said Grabo in a tone intended to grab the man's complete attention, body and soul. Borbor Pain turned to him. "Why didn't you tell all those people out there you were not a madman and that you were in fact a corporal in the army?"

"You don't get it, Grabo. I'm indeed a madman. I have to put up with that label because of the power in me. It was painful for me to see kids half-naked in the streets calling me a madman. Sometimes I felt like stopping my street illusion, but I couldn't. In a way, Grabo, I am happy that I am sitting here free from being considered mad now."

The loud speaker sounded again, this time carrying the voice of the man who had earlier been seen embracing Raster. He asked everyone to move closer to him so that they all stood as a family. He paused to allow his words to take effect. Borbor Pain and Grabo had not planned to move any closer, but soon the speaker was lost behind the heads of the crowd. And the applause was inviting. The two men found a place to stand where they could see right into the speaker's mouth.

"Fellow Kaibarans," the speaker resumed his speech. "My name is Dr. Manure Gallon. Many of you remember me as a man who served his country, beginning with the governments of the first two Prime Ministers, to the first executive president of our land. I have held important positions which, over the years, have exposed me to the problems and solutions of our beloved Kaibara. Those who know me well will tell you I love all of you as individuals and as my countrymen and women, but I love my country more."

Gallon paused to look about him and size up the hundreds of people listening to him. He gazed out at them with the conviction that he was helping to make a noble history for his people, a history long overdue.

The veins of his throat danced beneath a long chin. Indeed, Gallon was no stranger to podiums.

Many could remember that he had stood at over a hundred podiums. He had been around for a long time now. He was already a public figure when the British handed the nation its independence. Early on in that era, Gallon had earned a reputation as a man who could move a crowd and get them to move a mountain.

"Many of you still don't know why you are here. You have been dragged from the environments you know very well, that provided you comfort, that is if there is any comfort left in this country today, and have been brought to this strange place. Mark my words: if Kaibara will not develop until someone is discomforted, then I challenge you all to consider yourselves lucky, for being discomforted means you are the chosen few."

He looked around him again to emphasize the truth of his statement. A loud applause rang out in the woods. It was an appropriate hour to invoke a thunderstorm.

"Enough is enough! Kaibara needs a change. Whether you are here today or not, the hour of change has come. This government must be replaced. I will tell you why Jepehun has been chosen as the ground for this august body. You all know about *ndogbowusu*? Well if you do, I can only tell you today that what you know of it is the spirit of this gathering," Manure Gallon concluded, before thanking his audience, bowing, and stepping away from the podium.

Raster took the mike and coughed into it, wiped his lips, and cleared his throat. His lanky posture explained nothing. He fidgeted with his shirt and blew a cold greeting into the mike. A wild response came from the back where the notorious college students gathered. During the escape from prison, all one hundred and twelve students had stayed together, on their way to Jepehun, eight of them had died under the guns of government forces.

Raster introduced himself as the former president of the National Union of Students who had caused a whole lot of problems for the government of the first executive president of the land. From college campuses, he had called for that president's resignation. He said the president had become incapable of running the country. On more than one occasion, government security men had raided college campuses all over the country in search of him. Having failed to locate him, that executive president had dissolved students' union governments nationwide and had tried their erstwhile leader for treason in absentia.

"Unless you have never heard of that eternal student riot against the government, you will always remember the name of Raster Mohammed."

The students applauded him again and shouted, "Go Raster! Go Raster!"

Raster eagerly complied. "Many of us have not forgotten the many injustices suffered by defenseless Kaibarans then. Parents sent their children to college with the hope that they would be useful citizens in their country, and the government found pleasure in slaying them like hogs. We took to the streets of RoMarong City, peacefully protesting against the evils of the government. We sat on our college campuses

71

requesting dialogue with the government that we had voted into office to serve us. We wrote in the papers to register our opposition to the ruthlessness of the government. We called for a sense of nationalism. The president and what he called a government ganged up on us and chased many of us out of our own country.

"Today, we, the university students of that time who stood against the dictatorship of the government, are here with you to continue our good intention of freeing this fine country of ours from the talons of these dictators. This same spirit led us to help free five hundred university students unjustly taken from their college campuses and locked away in Dembapa prison.

"The death of the first president has not changed our country for the better because he saw it fit to put on our head a liability in the person of the second president who thinks he can   play chess on our heads. Ours is the first country in the history of man in which a leader could admit that he has failed his people and then be allowed to continue ruling them. Tell me where else has this ever happened?"

As the crowd erupted in applause, Borbor Pain felt his blood rushing through his veins. He dove inward to suppress the tightness that was gathering in the pit of his stomach. He pushed outward and arranged a grin on his face. He must combat whatever it was that wanted to disrupt him from listening to the young man. Raster's declamation was not strange to him. No, it was the way he put it. It was the spirit he attached to it that moved Borbor Pain, and, on the whole, he approved of him. "That's the way to go," he said to himself but loud enough for Grabo to hear.

"He talks well," Grabo said.

"I remember a rhyme I learned in school," continued Raster. "I still recite it today because I find it very appropriate for the duty I have to perform. This rhyme keeps reminding me about time and about the images of doom that lie ahead. And unless I address these problems, the simple rhyme repeats in my head, telling me about the end of days and the lurking darkness. However, as I enter into the night, I'm warned about shadows of the evening spreading still across the sky. *Aluta Continua!*" he shouted as he threw three punches in the air.

Raster was so dramatic that even after he had left the stage, the applause continued. By this time, the worn out crowd burned with fire, although the sun passed overhead quietly without anyone noticing. When Grabo caught it disappearing behind the foliage of the woods, its lingering rays produced a brilliant sky that held the impatient darkness at bay. Later the wind moved in whispers as though it knew not to disturb the trees or the gatherers on this portentous occasion.

"I said it all in RoMarong City, and when they heard me, they said to one another, 'This is a madman.'"

Borbor Pain was the one speaking into the mike from the podium. No one had seen him walk to the front, much less take the mike. Grabo had been looking at the sun and was startled to see Borbor Pain at the podium. Many others instantly remembered him as the madman under the cotton tree, but to others he was an

73

entertainer, and for this reason the crowd shouted with excitement and support. The applause that greeted him was far more enthusiastic than that given to either Manure Gallon or Raster Mohammed.

"But you all know that madness has become a drink manufactured and sold today in RoMarong City," said Borbor Pain. "Let us call it *ormole*. Political *ormole*. What I don't know is why the Catholic Church has not ordered that this drink be used to represent the blood of Christ. This drink is so potent that it has turned a whole nation upside down. It came about after the president partook of it during one of his lunch breaks. No sooner had he sipped it than he called all the important chiefs and confessed to them he had failed the nation. Don't you think the Catholic Church needs to serve this *ormole* during congregational confessions? It leads to confession!"

The support for Borbor Pain rang out loud in the forest and excited the birds. The white and Arab men who were standing off by themselves drew closer.

The Arabs first burst out laughing, and then the white men before the rest of the crowd picked it up.

As Borbor Pain replaced the mike, a wild applause filled the air. The white and Arab men reached for his hand and shook it in turns. He was enthusiastically led to join them where they had gathered. The two white ladies offered him big smiles.

However, for a moment, he wished to be left alone. He moved further away as though he were carrying some contagious cough. He shook his head vehemently and found himself subduing his inner intruder who he was sure had tempted him to assume the mike. After a short while, he was fine. He looked the rocks and then at the crowd where he made out Grabo. His friend was busy talking to another man who was somehow making him happy. The next speaker who assumed the mike announced food and drinks. Almost at once, two white vans emerged from the woods and stopped in the middle of the crowd. Some women alighted and began to remove containers of food and drinks. The crowd quickly moved over to them, ready for a feast.

6

"You may join us at table under that tree, Mr...."

"Corporal," Borbor Pain said, cleared his throat, and smiled. He felt airplanes flying in his head.

It was one of the Arab men who had tapped him on his shoulder and invited him to join the group under the tree. The man walked ahead of him and joined his colleagues who were already seated. Manure Gallon and Raster Mohammed were in the group. Borbor Pain looked around again and tried to locate Grabo in the crowd, but he couldn't find him. He's probably squatted somewhere over some dish, Borbor Pain thought. Everybody was moving up and down to secure food. It was their first meal since the gruesome trip from RoMarong City. Dishes and plates, spoons and cups, hands and sticks flew in the air as the sharing began.

76

"This looks like the business I have waited for all my life!" Borbor Pain turned and walked to the table he had been invited to join.

There a chair was waiting for him. Two tables had been brought together to accommodate all of them. They were covered with a white mackintosh that made every dish on them conspicuous. Borbor Pain counted three big dishes full of rice, three more of assorted stews and a daiquiri of other kinds of foodstuffs. The two white women were busy serving the Arab and white men. Manure Gallon and Raster Mohammed served themselves. An assortment of sodas and water in frost containers stood behind Borbor Pain.

Borbor Pain reminded himself that he was a vegetarian and would, therefore, need to choose his meal carefully. He wiped his hands on his prison uniform while he contemplated on what to do. He caught sight of a plate that was full of fruits when he reached for an apple, one of the Arab who had invited him to the table reached out and scooped up two apples and brutally took a bite.

"Mmhmh! I like it whichever way, either before or after a meal. Other times more creatively," the Arab looked into Borbor Pain's eyes. "Or rather I'll say I like to sandwich my meal." He reached again for two more apples and then, turning to one of the ladies at the table, he said, "Tiffany, tell me in which of the soup have you buried your pigs before I enter the wrong bowl?"

"You're probably finished with them by now. I see none on the table, and they were right in front of you. A change of diet, Macknoon?"

"Haram, haram! I told you my hands tell me when I hold anything I shouldn't eat. The cry of the pig is the beginning of every Muslim's pity," Macknoon said with his mouth full. He turned and found Borbor Pain still staring. "Hey, Corporal, after that speech I should definitely want to devour the whole table if I were you. Help yourself, man!"

"Like you, I too have to be careful picking my food."

"Oh, I see. Are you Muslim?"

"I'm vegetarian," Borbor Pain said.

Macknoon wasn't satisfied with the answer. Borbor Pain could be vegetarian all right, but what religion did he belong to for which he was vegetarian? Macknoon believed a man defined himself through his religion. "Vegetarian? You mean like Muslims not eating pig? Do you pray as a Vegetarian Muslim or a Vegetarian Christian?"

Borbor Pain gave him a wry smile, "I mean like vegetarian not eating meat and sticking to that, like a vegan vegetarian."

"Like a vegan? Whoa! We are really diverse in this small room of an earth. What is vegan?"

"Vegans go a little higher than vegetarians. I am a bit of both of them. Vegans, like vegetarians, don't eat meat, but beyond that they do everything to oppose meat eating and protect anything flesh and blood."

Just then Manure Gallon noisily opened one of the containers and brought out a chicken leg. Everyone burst out laughing.

"I guess you are in the wrong table, Mr. Vegan," Manure Gallon said. "You definitely won't like to see how I treat this one."

"My own case is not as unaccommodating as others," said Borbor Pain. "I don't have a human feeling for animals. I guess my concern is rather against cruelty, and cruelty comes not in your eating that chicken but in your killing it. Even then, it is the purpose and manner of killing it. Killing to eat is acceptable to me."

"Well, I guess if we had known that," said Tiffany, "we would have created a Berlin Wall at this table. We would have arranged the food fittingly, and I think we still have time to do so. What do you think, Susan?"

"I think that it would be less appetizing to rearrange the table at this point. It will be good if I announced the table setup and have people swap places."

"Susan is absolutely right," Raster said. "We want to be as accommodating as possible with every eating right expressed to satisfaction. I see myself between Janis and Brian." He was referring to the two white men.

"I will be with Mr ..." Tiffany started.

"Corporal, do you mean?" Macknoon said.

"Call me Corporal; that's enough."

"I'll be with Corporal. I'm seasonal in my belief. Today I choose to be a vegetarian but not a vegan though," Tiffany said.

Everyone laughed as Tiffany moved over to sit near Borbor Pain. The others made their preferences and sat accordingly. All soon had a plate full of their choices.

The noise of the crowd continued in the background. Spirits rose higher as occasional laughter erupted from among small groups. Half way into his food, Raster took his plate and began to walk about the table.

"Corporal, we are happy to get you around us," Raster said to Borbor Pain with his mouth full. "As you can see, we are all one big family. We've hung out together for a long time, and we are all together in what we stand for."

"That's good to hear. I felt that as soon as I joined you. This table has a way of making Vegans go seasonal like Tiffany," Borbor Pain said.

Everyone laughed again.

"We've been together for some four years now planning things," Brian, one of the white men, said. "I guess that makes us Kaibarans like you. Well, we all know things are pretty messy in RoMarong City. Some of us still remember the good report of Kaibara in the outside world. It doesn't take long to survey what's going on in a small country like Kaibara."

"Look, Corporal, you and Manure have been around for a long while now and have been deeply angered by the things happening in RoMarong City," Raster said. "We don't think it's fair that we sit by and see things going wrong."

"I found your speech very provoking, the way you made it, Corporal," Susan said. "Tell me, do you make speeches around? You could bring down a whole insecure government the way you talk."

Everyone agreed with Susan. Tiffany even added that she was thinking about becoming a vegan, which probably would give her the power Borbor Pain had.

Borbor Pain laughed and briefly told her she could be a steadfast vegan if she began by saving the lives of ants. His suggestion didn't make sense to Tiffany.

"Susan, you asked me if I make my speeches around. No, I don't. I make them straight."

There was laughter again.

"Why do you think a man like the Corporal was in prison?" asked Macknoon as he reached for two big slices of pineapple. "It is because he broke down an entire government."

"I've been in trouble with this government since the day it was founded," said Borbor Pain. "I know Mr. Manure, and he is a man for whom I have great respect. He may not remember me now, but if I remind him that I was the second accused in the first military coup against the government and the fifth accused in the second, he probably would begin to open his eyes."

"That's right!" shouted Raster. "I thought I have seen your face before! I was the students' union president then, and I had said over the BBC that the government had no right in detaining you for more than twenty four hours without trial. Your beard was not as silver and plentiful as it is now."

"Maybe I've been a vegan for too long. I thank God that it is not yet gray."

Everyone again laughed out loud.

By this time, the crowd in the background was entertaining itself with music. Puffs of smoke spiraled in the air as cigarettes and marijuana were passed around in abundance. Palm Wine and beer were also passed around.

"We can't believe how many diamonds go out of this beautiful country every day and yet people are so poor," said Janis the other white man who had remained quiet until now. "I don't know why I'm saying this, but unless someone saves Kaibara, these diamonds will soon become a curse to everyone."

"I see, you white men have interest in our diamonds, *eh*?" said Borbor Pain. "Am I right? That's why you are involved in whatever this is all about?"

Borbor Pain had dropped a rotten egg.

The table went silent. The implication was discomforting, the reality of it biting. Tiffany uttered a dark smile. Susan giggled and drank from an empty cup. Brian reached for a cigarette. Macknoon contorted his face, withdrawing his hands from the fruit bowl. Manure lowered his chicken leg. Raster froze in his seat. The night had almost relieved the day. The last rays of the sun coiled behind the foliage.

"Let's say you've hit the nail on the head, Corporal," said Raster replacing his plate on the table and pouring himself a glass of wine. "That's why we have you on this table and not out there dining with the rest. We are looking for a team. We want positive Kaibarans who can join us to usher in a change. We must use our diamonds to improve the way our country looks to the rest of the world. After all, that's why God blessed us with the valuable stones."

"Brian here and the other white guys you see are just what we need to realize our dream in the West," said

82

Manure. "Macknoon's team is selling our plans in the East."

"Ah, so I was sitting with the three wise men?" Borbor Pain observed, easing the tension.

"And with a wise woman," Tiffany added.

They all exploded with laughter and overturned with jokes.

Borbor Pain accepted a cigarette from Macknoon who lit it and took one long drag before handing it over to him. Without examining the make, Borbor Pain wedged it between his lips and left it to dangle there for a while. He wasn't really a smoker, but moments like these called for sharing, and little things such as turning down the offer of a cigarette could put a strain on a new relationship. In fact, Macknoon had laid out the packet he carried and instructed Borbor Pain to help himself to a few more. It was then he learned that the brand was an Arab one. It was Borbor Pain's first time smoking an Arab made cigarette.

Borbor Pain saw Raster and Brian whispering to each other and decided they didn't really like him. Manure helped himself to a bottle of whisky that Macknoon had half emptied. Borbor Pain wondered whether Macknoon had a religious or health reason for drinking whiskey like he had for not eating pigs. The two white women fondled with each other's hair as they discussed something Borbor Pain couldn't hear. Macknoon and his Arab countryman kept taking Borbor Pain back to his speech. However, they were actually discussing the president, whom the Arabs for some reason after his declaration that he had failed the nation, thought had suddenly been incapacitated.

Borbor Pain again cast his eyes on the crowd in search of Grabo, but he couldn't penetrate the rowdy throng. He thought Grabo was probably about asking after his wife in *gara* and some funny head-tie. Somehow he felt lucky that he didn't have the problem of a wife to worry about. He recalled his estranged wife who had eloped with a man known to have carried a dilapidated briefcase around referring to himself as a doctor. It all happened three years after the birth of their only child. His wife had abandoned the child in the care of an indifferent aunt.

Everyone in their village knew the story, but it wasn't the villagers' business to tell a husband who was never there for his wife. Borbor Pain had been in the habit of leaving the village to as he would tell his wife, attend political meetings in RoMarong City. His wife never understood why her husband couldn't play politics among his own townspeople as other politicians did, nor did she understand why he always went away to who knew where.

She had cried for one full month after he had abandoned her. She was told her husband had been implicated in a coup plot in the city and would very likely be hanged there. Relatives who visited her gave her hope that she would see him again, but she had heard the same people saying to others that Borbor Pain would never again be a free man, even with the best lawyer at his disposal. Borbor Pain for that matter could not afford the best lawyer or any lawyer except the one provided by the state. So it happened that Borbor Pain spent six months in prison following the foiling of the second coup. He was lucky to have been one of three accused later to be freed. He of course lost his job in the military and returned to his wife in the village empty handed.

His wife had already shed all the sorrow in her and had learned to love another man. Borbor Pain walked into a house that didn't expect him. He returned with infinite misery and torment. He could not afford to support his wife because he had no job. The briefcase doctor had been visiting the village every weekend. He could be found in the village square displaying his drugs and musically explaining illnesses they cured. The villagers bought many drugs and consulted with him on how to consume them.

While Borbor Pain was in prison, his wife had fallen ill regularly from all those bitter tears she had shed every night. Her head began troubling her. The briefcase doctor had learned about her ordeal. Because he felt sorry for her, he gave her free drugs. He also helped follow up on her husband, Borbor Pain's court case in the city. Every time he returned to the village, he reported to her that the trial was on, but that people were keeping tight lipped about it. In turn for his sacrifice, Borbor Pain's wife offered him water and a seat on her verandah so that he could rest after his tiring day of sales. Then he began leaving money behind for spicy weekend pepper soup.

Borbor Pain had returned to the village hoping his wife would support him. He spoke about how lucky he was to be alive while ten others, all very important people, were hanged. He explained his ordeal as a noble feat and wanted his wife to know that he had ignited the engine of greatness! But his wife wasn't impressed. Years after she eloped with the briefcase doctor, Borbor Pain returned to RoMarong City as a vagabond living under the city central cotton tree.

"Corporal—I hope you don't mind my addressing you so," said Raster approaching him.

"As a matter of fact, those who know me well address me that way."

"I have just had a lengthy discussion with Dr. Manure, and you have been the subject of our discussion," he pulled up a chair.

"To be the subject of a discussion is nothing. It is the topic," Borbor Pain said.

It struck Raster that Borbor Pain had made a sharp and witty statement. He was convinced the corporal was indeed made of enough jungle stuff to pound the hell out of the enemy.

"Our friends and Dr. Manure think highly of you," Raster said.

Borbor Pain smiled. "I'm flattered, Mr. Mohammed, but if I may ask, what is this all about?"

"That is it. That is what you are about to know shortly, but you can rest assured that we are brothers. For now though, we will all leave the woods for another place. It is getting darker here."

"Mr. Mohammed!" Borbor Pain called with a sharp change of tone in his voice. It brought the others at the table to attention as they all turned and stared at him.

"I have to say this. You and your men are holding us hostage! And whatever your idea is, I find this very distressing."

Dr. Manure rose from his chair in one big leap and walked over to him. "I have no doubt you understand what this is all about by now, Corporal. I believe your question should be, 'where do I come in here?' If you are patient, you'll soon find out, corporal."

Borbor Pain saw Grabo in the crowd. He turned to Dr. Manure and said, "If you'll excuse me, doctor? I see my friend. We've been looking for each other since the briefing broke off."

Borbor Pain walked away. Manure was impressed with his choice of words. He felt Borbor Pain spoke like the seasoned soldier he knew him to be long years ago: "since the briefing broke off." Hearing the expression, Manure realized Raster's foresight in suggesting that the rally be planned and carried out just as it had been.

While they had been outside the country planning this initial recruitment, Manure had cast doubts on what he called Raster's idealistic program being spread between RoMarong City and Jepehun. How could that stretch of more than two hundred miles support such a dangerous program without exposing the entire agenda?

Raster had insisted it would be the only way to create the impact that was needed. Manure explained to their foreign partners the cartographic risk involved. He had suggested the initial recruitment be limited to Jepehun. However, they had a limited time to keep debating on the networking aspect of the program. Their financiers wanted to know what was happening. At first, the partners thought targeting RoMarong City's Dembapa Prison at that initial stage was risky and ambitious, so they had agreed at that meeting it had to begin with Jepehun while they prepared themselves for RoMarong City.

But just the other week (and for this reason the program had been shifted to one week later) news had reached Raster that the government had arrested over a hundred students and thrown them into prison to die. With this new development, Raster reorganized the whole plan and requested that RoMarong City be included in their initial drive. Although the partners instantly approved, Manure still had his fears. He'd had the task of recruiting members in Jepehun. He recruited his crowd in two days. He remained jittery about the RoMarong City program to the last day. His spirit had just begun to sink when Raster appeared with truckloads of escapees from the Dembapa Prison. Manure had welcomed Raster with a warm embrace and a high spirit.

Dr. Manure Gallon stood six feet, two inches in height. His lanky body hid much of his age within his solid bones. He was a man who had too much to say and said it in too many words. He believed too much in having a confidant who automatically passed for his friend. It was in that circumstance that he had met Raster fifteen years earlier.

There was a time when Manure considered himself a vanguard of his country's independence even though he wasn't actually a politician. He was, in fact, out of the country somewhere in Britain, locked within four walls of books when the nation's founding fathers had stormed the Queen's palace requesting independence.

When Manure returned home years later, he quickly found his way into his people's hearts through his medical profession. He joined the ruling party. Although many notables in the party preceded Manure, yet the government managed to make him a minister because he wanted a medical doctor to head the department of health. Years later, Manure betrayed his party after it was narrowly defeated in a general election. He double-crossed his boss and gave his allegiance to the new ruling party, which at first didn't countenance him, but after he opted to become the personal physician of the president, he bought himself a cabinet position in the next shakeup.

Borbor Pain hooked up with Grabo. He had found him in the company of Bassie, the warden who had removed their shoes from their feet when they first went to Dembapa Prison. There were a dozen men who wanted to meet him. Grabo introduced them to him and him he introduced as The Corporal. Reaching for his hand, one after the other, the men said great speakers never need any introduction. Grabo kept assuring them that Borbor Pain was flattered. He had met them in the middle of a conversation about the president's confession of failing the nation. He excused himself from the group and asked to talk to Grabo privately. As they walked away, one of the men in the group shouted to them.

"The Corporal, you and your men must be sure we are here for you. We are ready to offer body and soul for the course."

Borbor Pain turned to Grabo and asked what was going on.

"*You* should tell *me*, Corporal. I wonder why I never knew that you had co-staged two military coups against the government," he paused and continued, "Don't you notice that the crowd has been divided into small groups? For the past hour, units of men have been telling us why we are here."

"And just what did they say?" Borbor Pain asked.

"I don't get it. They spoke so highly of you and the other people sitting with you at table. They told us you all had one mind." He paused and stared at him. "Now are you going to tell me why you hid the whole thing from me?"

"What are you talking about? Hid what from you?" Borbor Pain couldn't help laughing.

"Are you not one of these guys? Did you not plan it with them?"

"No, I didn't! What's going on here?"

"Well, whatever it is that has happened, everyone has been told to look up to you, because they—I don't get it—they are preparing us for war—against the government."

Raster walked up behind them and tapped Borbor Pain on the shoulder.

"Corporal, a word with you," Raster said.

"Meet my friend, Grabo," Borbor Pain said, as though he had not heard Raster's request. "We came from

RoMarong City together. Do you want him to excuse us?"

"Oh, no, it's okay. He can stick around. I am happy to meet you Grabo." When Raster stretched out his hand, Grabo took it and nodded respectfully.

Turning to Borbor Pain, he said, "We are all about to leave this place—you and me and, well, Grabo and all the others on the high table," Raster said, mentioning Grabo as if to justify why he should listen to what he had to say. "We are crossing over the border. Grabo and the other guys will stay there while you, our foreign friends, and I will head for Libya tonight. You'll like it. It's a beautiful country," Raster tapped him again. "You'll like every bit of what we are doing."

"How do you feel about this, Grabo?" Borbor Pain turned a confused face to his friend.

Grabo quickly gathered himself and snapped to attention so stiffly that he hurt his leg. Ignoring the pain, he saluted and opened his mouth to speak. "What are we waiting for? All is correct, Sir!"

The narrator suspected that I was losing concentration, but more frighteningly, that the pillar of cloud had moved considerably from under me. Only a thin veil of cloud remained, and already in fear, I was beginning to look below me. Realizing that I could fall from more loss of cloud, he tapped me on the shoulder, and in that instant we began to descend to earth, back to New York, the city of my exile.

7

By the middle of the 1990s the taste of my exile had completely mixed with that of my nostalgia. Voluntary retirement in New York City was a second exile for me: exile from action without being inactive. Moreover, I used it as a yardstick to approximate and appreciate the city filled with large surging crowds with their shoes flopping against the tired streets. Every day, I felt the echoes of New Yorkers' numerous sweeping shoes on the pavements until I found myself in bed at night and locked in a stranglehold of dreams. I always thought myself lucky that such a prancing city didn't jump on my head or come crashing down on top of me after all the years I spent there.

New York City and exile were twin cities of my twin selves. Regularly, I was brought to acknowledge that I had crossed over with my psyche from New York City to the City of Exile. Better said, I had romanticized New York into that other city. The answer I gave those curious enough to ask about me, though indeed they were few, depended on the concern I sensed coming from their eyes. Over time, I became attached to Exile as much as to New York, long after my city of birth, RoMarong City, had abandoned me, and my country, Kaibara, had thrown me out, vomiting me onto the backwaters of the oceans of Africa.

In Exile, as in New York, there were no corridors, no foyers, only inner and outer curves that ran haphazardly into one another to form confused overheads of worrisome squares. The tiny, black legs upholding unintelligible notice boards filled with instructions, some written in cardinal characters, stretched through the outskirts of the two cities, ran into neighboring cities, and met again at some intersection where the two turned into monsters and growled at each other.

The two cities both evolved into concepts about the height of urban closure. I believed they were cities of technocracy with road networks stretching into super highways and, finally, turning inward into minds and outward into garbage. In these two cities, I saw people musing and feeding on silence.

Every musing came from people, whose hands always occupied their pockets, walking down some lonely avenue. I myself was regularly lonely in crowds of people, some of which had very noisy accents. Perambulating the city squares, I counted over twelve dozen accents, each trying to create its own English.

I came to New York when Anglo-Saxons dominated it, and all other accents sounded like bees closing in on their botanical targets. I rarely encountered the "first nations," the so-called American Indians, who had been busy depositing the rural souls of their departed ones in the land they once called theirs. Of course, I soon learned that New York was not the kind of place Indians would like to call their own for the simple reason that everyone called them Indians, a name they so hated, but more so because New York lacked a spiritual mode.

In the winter, when all accents groped for warmth in metro buses, I heard the somber arrangements of their rhythms accompanying the cry of automobiles under the pacific effects of traffic lights.

When I spoke, I was frequently reminded to slow down if, say, I was asking a hunch-backed woman for directions. "Please, I cannot keep up with your accent," she would say.

I quickly learned that with language I had to go in the fashion of parallel colors on the super highway demarcated by unbroken yellow lines. Nevertheless, eventually all accents seemed to merge as if directed by a bewildering complex of traffic signs. Or did they create the foundation of some super juncture where memory and association formed the structure of pillars holding up the communications highway? New York was as musical as American Jazz and as colorful as a rainbow.

Each season arrived with certain assurances and with a cultivated hope that someday I was going to belong.

Already Harlem was opening its doors by the Ghetto Square to the Hispanic and other minorities. Harlem became a haven for Spanish and the other languages that were heard only in winter telephone booths. Harlem spoke Spanish (not just the words) fluently because Spanish was a mortal body and a language for the oppressed to cry in.

A new protective pyramid emerged, sepulchral and imposing, and soon all non-Anglo-Saxons carved their own niches to define themselves in colored terms within the frontiers of the world's most animalistic city. New York thus proved that the majority of minorities could effect a change.

Harlem also discovered the Nubian in the African immigrant. Most Black Americans, as they then called themselves, believed that the thick crust black skin of the African represented what God had in mind when he thought of human beings because to them Eden was an African garden. Black Americans also regarded Black Africans as the chosen ones, closer in nature to God than any other people walking the earth.

It was common to hear them say, "Brother, you're the real child of God, the real black man. You know what I'm saying? You're from Nubia, where black people built a civilization. I love you, brother."

However, I found all the expectations too heavy to carry. I longed to set every record straight. I knew how I wanted to say things, although I never came to say them. Instead I ended up shouting inside my own head: "I'm not from Nubia—from Africa, yes! I'm from Africa but from another place in Africa. Africa is a continent three times bigger than the United States! I'm from the West Coast where great empires also rose. My people never knew Egypt when they built their own civilization. I'm not Nubian!"

But what difference did it make to a people desperately trying to understand a lost ethos? Soon Black American businesses began displaying the Nubian expression on their business signs. There were the "Nubian Enterprises," "Nubian International," and "Island Nubian Records."

My British colonial education created a black British ethic within me that admonished me to hold sacred the language and the royalty. I had lost my claim to the new language. I'd overdosed on British colonialism enough to grant me authority to frown at the way Americans conducted themselves. However, I soon saw myself as embarrassingly interposed between the British flag and the American argument. My first American roommate claimed that America was still rebelling against the lexical trappings of the English monarchy. I was aware of the language war between the two peoples. Alistair Cook in his BBC *Letter from America* once said, "As for the Americans, they haven't spoken English in years."

Nevertheless, it wasn't for me to say as much, since I was only a British subject of African descent seeking refuge in the New World. In those days, it was common for people with strange accents to be asked when they intended going back home. Later, whenever I stood before a mirror and beheld my twin self without having decided where I belonged in the house of Exile,

I actually asked the man in the mirror when he really intended to go back home.

I knew better than to fool myself into believing that I would return to a Nubia. I realized that even if I were Nubian, with the memory of the full panoply of that empire's civilization, I had no Nubia to return to now. My Nubia, my real Nubia on the West Coast of Africa, had long been conquered by a peculiar kind of Egyptian led by oversized countrymen who thought strange things. I wondered whether the fact that Africans, from the Congo to the Gold Coast, were abusing their political independence meant anything to Harlem.

Did the cavernous buildings of New York stir by night and find themselves displaced in the morning? Or was I the one who moved in the morning and found myself displaced at night? A fear grew inside me that I would one day find myself squeezed inside a pit. I had carried too much of my country in my heart and didn't realize that in New York I inevitably had room enough for only my race and color. Other times, I suffered the phantasmal phobia of being in a race with the millions of other New Yorkers, and amidst the forlorn excitement, something indigenously atavistic would pull me back or trip me up. My evenings always ended in displacement. Soon, I began to drag the universal chain of being black in the place of my specific Kaibaran identity.

I was born in a city very unlike New York. RoMarong City woke each morning with a meticulous privacy and full of heart. The buildings were not dark. They were not tall, and they didn't march about. They knelt quietly in communal fashion and spread their narrow palms for the populace to traverse. This city slept at night and was always in time to wake me in the morning with its plumage fanning me its gentle breeze. Unlike New York, RoMarong City was always disposed to seeing its residents through the day. The city accompanied me by day and followed the fluctuations of my imagination; by night, it shared my bed with me. It was the pride of my country in a tormented continent. It was Nubian in all respects. RoMarong City glowed with wonder. Each year, for example, I saw other Africans rapt with appreciation of my country's university, which constituted the African version of Athens couched in the first European citadel of learning in colonial Africa. Other Africans who came seeking knowledge drank from my country's Perian spring to provide succor to their countrymen in unfortunate regions of the continent.

Yolanda had never stopped preaching to me that idleness made me susceptible to all kinds of thoughts. I had just stepped down from the only job I had held in New York these thirty-odd years. Was I prepared to concentrate my efforts on constantly dreaming about a country that had long forgotten me? Born in the heart of New York, all Yolanda had gathered about my years in Kaibara from her mother was that I was committed to my job at the expense of my marriage.

Her mother had persuaded her to believe her propaganda, not through words but by the tears that ran down her face each night as they sat together before the television screen awaiting my late return. She told her many other things about my past, which had all come back to me, thanks to the Socratic minds of children.

When my wife had announced her intention to divorce me, I was not surprised that Yolanda chose to go with her. In fact, I had fully expected her to team up with her mother and try to force me out of the house. A friend who lived in Manhattan once told me in a drunken stupor, after his own wife walked out of his life one night, "Any man who loses his wife in New York must hold the city responsible. Nowhere are women corrupted more easily than in this city. And you must be lucky if your wife walks out of your life without a loaded gun. But you know what? The only good thing about New York is that it's too athletic to turn one into a passive divorcee. In any case, I'm suing the city for distressing me."

The next day my friend was found dead at the outskirts of the city. He had forgotten that New York City was still the vertiginous place that Mickey Spillane, had written about so many times in cadaverous prose.

Earlier, before my wife moved out, I had wondered what she had meant when she told me there was nothing anyone could do about a country in the middle of a war. Had she conceived a marital breach when I made known my intention to resume my unfinished journey as a politician in Kaibara? I was aware my intention to return to Kaibara to re-establish my law firm had troubled her. She had often told me it was a disturbing dream to her. She had taken to conversing with me in psychiatric terms—the effect, I thought, of caring for old people who sat in wheelchairs reliving their lives through confessions.

When she drove on Route 495, she got trapped in the shoes of her patients. Her agency was aware of her vulnerability and so it preferred her to be the initial contact for their assisted living home programs in the musicality of emergencies.

At first, I dragged my feet about the divorce although I had agreed to it only because I believed she needed some time for that tormenting bird to fly from her heart. I thought I reacted the way a man who didn't want a divorce should react. However, she had a nagging way of reminding me about it, so one day I brought with me a thick envelope and dropped it before her. The next day I returned home to find a deserted apartment, a disregarded divorce application form, and a telephone message:

"I moved out, Desmond. You could call it a separation. Let's leave it at that. You wanted it yourself anyway."

"Good," I had thought, believing that a separation would give her the time to think it over.

I couldn't go to work the next day. For the first time in over thirty years, America was my wifeless home. Apparently, as I would later come to know, she had been discussing her home affair with her patients who had advised her how to treat such a husband. The day she moved out, the apartment magically expanded, creating a room where there was none before, creating a void in the space where she had taught our daughter to nag about one thing or the other. *It is better to stay alone*

100

than with a nagging and complaining woman! The voice of the Bible teaches. Should I say no? Three nights after my wife and daughter were gone, the phone rang again!

"I have no doubt that you understand why Mum has done this," Yolanda began.

I thought my daughter was crazy, but I believed she was being pressured. Or do all women behave that way?

"Wait a minute, even the good Lord has some doubts. Where in his name have you two gone to live? How can you both just walk away from me like that?"

Wasn't that how the head of a broken home should react? Patch things up desperately even when there are no bits left with which to patch?

Yolanda, ignoring my question, said "Dad, let's face it, Mum cannot stand your politics any longer. She thinks that you have always treated her like a vote."

"Like a vote? What are you talking about? How long has this nonsense been going on between the two of you? Look, put your mum on the phone. One moment, it's about my politics, and another moment it's about my long hours on the job."

A long pause ensued. I held the phone firmly to my ear. Yes, it would be good for my wife to come and talk to me from whatever world she had gone to.

"Will you let this pass for the night, Dad? Have a good night. I love you, Dad," Yolanda said and dropped the handset.

Was all of this game love or madness?

I shouted into the disconnected line, "Wait! Wait!" But there was no waiting on the other end.

So that was it. I could do nothing about a family in the middle of a war! For the eight years that followed, my wife and I didn't talk to each other, at least not directly. I never understood how Yolanda, at her innocent age, had stepped into the role of a go-between. However, the two of them were all I had, and if I wanted to discuss my broken home or catch up with its state, they were the only ones to whom I could turn.

My wife and I had enjoyed a very happy marriage for the better part of thirty years, but I later noticed that my frustration over the war in Kaibara took its toll on our marriage. Occasionally, when I gave some thought to it, I justified my wife's frustration. She could not understand why a man who had nearly lost his life and had endangered those of his wife and parents should be eager to return to the same doom in a country in the middle of a war. My long hours on the job had sounded like those horrible nights in Kaibara when I had returned home and told her that the president had held me back along with my colleagues at unending emergency meetings.

Before our separation, each evening on weekends I always sat with my wife long into the nights discussing the war when we heard it had broken out in the southern part of our beloved country. Information was scarce on the American television stations, and the papers mentioned the story only as a reference to the unending African predicament. It also provided backup information to the external effects of the civil war of a neighboring country that had erupted some two years earlier. The war in Kaibara had helped explain the madness of that country's warlord whom American journalists had taken to dissecting in their newspapers after discovering he had not only served terms in an American prison but also had escaped it armed with the best American mind their universities could offer.

The papers created a story with notable names from Arab countries looming large as supporters of a West African network meant to destabilize the region as long as it stayed free of American influence. However, little was known about the rebel movement that had just declared war on the central government. At one point, Yolanda came running to us with what looked like a computer animation of the fiery orator who had declared himself the leader of the rebellion. His name was Borbor Pain. He looked too disheveled to be taken for anything beyond a common beggar in the streets of RoMarong City or New York or, for that matter, Exile City. Yolanda's mother had instantly suggested that his bushy face explained the inherent downfall of his movement.

I had chided her for that suggestion. In that instant, the forceful adrenaline of history brought forth the memory of Borbor Pain. I must have crossed path with him regularly in RoMarong. Although he was an older man to me, yet I was still able to picture him in his military uniform when the names and faces of the accused persons were published following the ever first military coup that was foiled in Kaibara. I remembered that Borbor Pain had been lucky to have been one of three accused coup plotters to be freed while ten others were executed. I wondered whether in fact Borbor Pain knew that the president had gone after my life as a result of his military coup and that I was in exile because of him and his cohorts of coup plotters.

"Don't you see that the man is wearing the face of a prophet? Would you not regard his silver beard with some divine awe?" I had said to her, glad that at least someone was standing up to the devils that had sent me into exile and had held Kaibarans hostage all those years.

"Here it says the leader is a little known man who spat words instead of spoke them and did everything else out of neurotic excitement. Dad, do you recognize his face? Was this someone from *your* movement?"

I didn't like anyone calling a whole government a movement. "Movement" sounded more like the Boys Scouts than a political entity. It wasn't a movement; it was a government. Besides, I had known no other man of psychiatric imbalance such as my daughter described except my former boss, the then president. I found the president I had worked under more intolerable than my family had found Borbor Pain—to think that they knew the latter only in pictures. Nevertheless, I didn't reply to my daughter's question because I had long grown ashamed of associating myself with that aspect of my past.

My wife continued to stare at the photo. "This leader resembles some Arab merchant whose face conveys something of the Sahara desert. Is this some sort of a religious movement? And why would anyone want to convert Kaibara into an Islamic state?" she asked.

My wife couldn't contain what I angrily called her Christianized rage.

"I fear that is all there is to this war," she lamented. "Thank God we are far away from that mess."

I gave up trying to convince her about the good intention of Borbor Pain, even if he had problems in presenting himself as such.

Back in RoMarong my wife paid little or no attention to politics. Even when I tried to tell her who Borbor Pain was, she would not listen to me. As a matter of fact Borbor Pain and the others' second coup attempt which was a reaction to the president's machination to convert Kaibara to a one party system had also been responsible for the first incarceration of some of my closest friends in Freetown, like Archibald Cole. I was to learn that the president thought that some of his closest officers, including me had betrayed him by disclosing his real intention of keeping himself in power forever under a one party state.

My wife developed an instant distaste for the rebel leader and his movement. She referred to them as, "that Islamic movement in our country."

The reality was whoever knew Borbor Pain would not associate him with either Christianity or Islam. He was a self-made man.

Whenever she berated Borbor Pain, I felt a certain pity for my family. My wife and I had been away from Kaibara for too long to understand the operations there. The last time I remembered writing a letter to anyone in RoMarong City was some twelve years before the war. My wife and I had predicted in our letter to

Archibald that the president wouldn't last long in power. We believed that soon the people would want to take charge of their own affairs and would trust no one but their own children to run the country. Being in the United States, I was ready for the people's power and ready to halt the betrayal of independence by the dictator and his team because I had unfinished business with my enemies. For me, Borbor Pain was utilizing the only option to boot out the criminals posing as leaders in Kaibara.

My wife and I had predicted in our letter that all who betrayed the people would be captured and destroyed. We wrote of an impending revolution that would restore the good works of the colonial masters, and those few worthy to be considered founding fathers of their country's independence would be decorated. Our letter had been full of hope that we wouldn't stay long in the United States and would return home to continue our dream of nation building. Yolanda had just been born then.

That was the last letter my wife and I would jointly write to RoMarong City. Three weeks after we received his reply, Archibald Cole reportedly died in incarceration. Although the nature of his death was not explained, we feared he was killed because of implicating documents, such as our letters to him, found in his possession. Someone even mentioned that Archibald was long ago associated with the planning of the rebellion that eventually emerged with Borbor Pain as leader.

106

We waited and waited for political change, but all the news from RoMarong City spoke of terror and mysterious deaths organized by presidential thugs who went by such notorious name of Highway.

There were times when I felt my family hadn't really been there for me. Yolanda and her mother knew I had waited a long time and that all those I had run from were either dead or imprisoned. I expected my family to understand that I could now stand tall for all Kaibarans to see that I was right and had seen it all coming. A man of ambition needs all the support he can get, but my family made my goals looked foolhardy, like a walk into a dark alley full of knife-wielding thieves.

All they wanted was for me to abandon Kaibara. That was their mistake, of thinking that Kaibara was behind me these thirty-odd years. I guessed the parting point between my wife and I hinged on her refusal to identify with my cause. What meaning was left for me, then, in the saying that he who fights and runs away lives to fight another day? I really had to fight or forever considered myself dead! I also knew one other thing: America could never replace Kaibara in my heart and my esteem.

When I thought about the little conversations in which my family had engaged me and made me angry, I resolved that Kaibara too needed volunteers to teach its illiterate adults how to protect their resources and, what's more, how to part with them. Suddenly I felt a deep hunger for my native land, a hunger that carried with it the raw desire to shout within the footholds of those rude caves whose roars chased the colonialists away.

Kaibara needed volunteers to help illuminate the simple minds of my people, to generate anger in them. Scores of literacy support service agencies were needed in Kaibara to spark fire in my people. "Reading and writing are very effective weapons to tear a nation apart," was my lingering thought as expressed to a blank and spent fisherman who had sworn to deprive his own children of schooling in those corrupt times until I was allowed to participate freely in the affairs of my country. The innocent poor man was moved by my rhetoric as the canoe sailed to safety through the impenetrable darkness of our motherland thirty years ago at a time when my name tasted badly on the lips of those who had once called me comrade, countryman, and brother.

8

The narrator prepared me to be ready for the most violent part of his narration. He had read through me and realized that I was too much of a theoretician when it came to talking about wars. He was however determined that I received his narration just as hard as Kaibarans at home had received the civil war:

When the first shot of rebellion rang out in the woods of Jepehun the revolution began. The soporific villagers in the surrounding areas gathered their hearts in their palms as subsequent shots echoed across the land and through the farms to announce the beginning of dark episodes in their country.

The villagers had been speaking in fear about the border up by the gradient land that separated the two countries of Kaibara and its immediate neighbor. The small unit of policemen stationed on the border was commissioned to ward off the influence of battle from that neighboring country which was the first to experience a civil war.

The war still raged in the neighboring country. One of that country's sons had arisen to challenge the downward slope of everything the people had stood for. Their conflict was so thunderous that in the two years since the war began, it still shook all of its borders.

The shared border with Kaibara had collapsed with little resistance. Advancing like the wind, boisterous crowds came from across the border and cleared everything that demarcated the land. The border police took flight and never looked back, remembering only that they swore an oath to maintain peace, and not to look violence in its face and play the fool with it.

News of the cross border invasion into the country took a long time to reach RoMarong City. News had been delayed on the tongues of the policemen who thought that time would repel the attackers and allow the officers to return to their base where they accepted the bribes of sorrowful passengers in vehicular traffic who ventured out on the haunted road.

However, the invaders had time in their favor, time that had allowed them to pitch makeshift tents and to promulgate their presence with unruly gunfire. The waiting had been too long for the policemen and already the commercial effect of the road-block was a backward-blowing wind that affected the villagers. The once fearless traders who had carried food supplies

110

across the border to procure higher profits because the conflict sabotaged farming dared not to ply their trade any more.

The news had first traveled down to RoMarong City via traders who felt bitter over their economic loss and were now forced to divert their wares to their own countrymen living in the un-agricultural city of RoMarong. These traders vehemently grumbled over prices with their new customers whom they thought were lucky to see good palm oil and fresh bananas, mangoes, and oranges at a time when they ought to be in the hands of the people across the border who knew their worth. Soon news of the blockade circulated in the language of complaint all over RoMarong City.

Cognizant of the news leak, the police unit rose from its slumber and dashed to RoMarong City to report the incident, calling it simply a fresh, unprovoked attack of people who looked like rebels from the neighboring country, and who had fought their way through customs and immigration officers, after seizing the border and chasing all police and government officials away. The police however were able to escape, they said, leaving behind all they had worked for through their entire lives.

Three weeks after the attack, Borbor Pain, perfectly dressed in military finery with shiny badges and complex medals on his shoulders and chest, stood at the heart of Jepehun. He surveyed the length and breadth of the backwoods of Jepehun as though he wished to recreate the ridges that didn't quite channel the tributaries to the distant river between Kaibara and the neighboring country.

Inside a small hut that held the noisy wind at bay, Borbor Pain had just spoken into a microphone for twenty-five minutes, responding to questions from the man who held it before him. He spoke with thunder and eloquently got all his thoughts across. Finally the world was going to know about him and hear his story, and the world was going to learn to put up with him.

After the interview, he had asked the interviewer to replay his tape. He loved what he heard over the speaker. His voice carried his intended threats. He didn't trust his English for a broadcast as universal as the BBC; however, he convinced himself that what he had to say to the world was more important than how he said it.

Standing outside the hut some two hours after the interview, Borbor Pain, no longer referred to as the mad man, inspected an honor guard. Three thousand fifty men stood before him in utter silence. They had new Russian Kalashnikovs on their backs. The fiery voice of Borbor Pain shaped them. Like a doctor giving a general prescription to an illiterate patient, he always said to, "recruit more fighting men and women, boys and girls in the morning, at noon, and in the evening too."

Jepehun had welcomed Borbor Pain and his message of war. Borbor Pain and his men had been allowed to annex the town and its surrounding villages and to do with it as they saw fit. Borbor Pain had taken their goodwill in good faith. However, he was certain that

112

their permission had not counted much because he would have seized the town anyway. The town had long been identified as a strategic point to situate the new movement's headquarters. He still remembered that into this town he was marched straight from Dembapa Prison.

On this day, mothers were bringing their twelve to fifteen-year-old children to listen to the message of change. Someone with long gray beards had come from the "good old days" with a message of hope to mothers of tears, depressed husbands, lost children, and wretched kinsmen.

The townspeople declared a holiday in the name of their dumbfounded town chief. Teachers unhappy about their salary backlogs, students bored with the lessons of woe and inflation, and civil servants wearied with the emptiness that filled their tables, joined the crowd to listen to the "message of change" brought by the remarkable long-bearded soldier.

The man with the microphone moved about the crowd on the request of Borbor Pain. He was conspicuous, not because he carried a microphone but because he was a white man who went around introducing himself to people he wanted to interview as a reporter from the BBC. His presence boosted the spirits in the meeting, especially when Borbor Pain announced that he was the Director-General of the BBC.

Borbor Pain didn't need to prepare a speech. He had felt every pain he was going to tell the people about. He waited for a signal from the back before he took the

113

floor. His prompter, who had gone to ensure the loud speakers were evenly distributed to ensure that those far away got the message, was approaching from the back with two other men flanking him.   .

Borbor Pain always waited for him to give the signal. He relied on him for his good sense of organization. They had worked together for several years now and understood each other well. Since meeting in Dembapa Prison, Borbor Pain and Grabo Burnah had learned to support each other in screwing their bolts in a flawless motion that suggested longtime familiarity.

Years ago, Borbor Pain had been asked to join the group of Manure, Raster, and their foreign partners on their way to cross the border of the neighboring country in a Toyota Jeep. He had thanked Raster for allowing Grabo to be in the group. They had journeyed right through to the neighboring country whose rebels had agreed to team up with the new rebels of Kaibara.

While Grabo stayed behind in the neighboring country with some twenty-odd men and women, Borbor Pain was put into an airplane, along with Manure, Raster, and their partners, and flown first to another neighboring country before heading for Libya.

At a room booked for him in a Tripoli hotel, Borbor Pain spent a whole night talking with Raster and Manure. On their arrival they allowed Borbor Pain a good night's rest to recover from the long journey. He had told them it was his first time to travel on an airplane. They discovered he had been nervous and restless and had stayed awake all throughout the flight.

114

The following morning, Raster took him shopping around in Tripoli where he bought fine Libyan gowns that magically transformed him into a man of status. In his new clothes he was no longer the tattered man under the cotton tree or the uniformed Dembapa Prison inmate. He looked like a world executive heading a chain of international businesses. He loved his looks and told Raster so. Raster gave him some money in case he wanted to buy something.

Borbor Pain couldn't believe the transformations were taking place in his life. At first he had the odd feeling that nothing happening was real. He felt like he was having a vision similar to the one involving him and the president under the cotton tree in RoMarong City. But should this be really happening just because a few white and Arab folks thought he knew how to rouse a crowd? The clothes on his body, the dollars in his pocket which he occasionally removed to examine, and the country and people he was around continued to strike him as new phenomena. When nothing reverted to its former status, he realized he was no longer experiencing his visions.

When the partners first saw him in his new gown, they mistook him for some oil-rich Nigerian who had just stepped off his private jet to transact business in Tripoli. He moved closer to them. No sooner was he recognized than Macknoon and his team fell on him in joy and greeted his extraordinary appearance.

A frisky Libyan female attendant whose unusual manner of dress pattern had brought some ideas into Borbor Pain's head ushered him into a room. Raster jocularly assured him that his dollars could fetch him any kind of fun. Borbor Pain understood what he meant, but he wouldn't be drawn into that kind of discussion, especially because he didn't know if Raster was preying on his morality. Certainly he agreed that he needed some good time particularly when against his expectation, life seemed very secular in Libya. He would know exactly what to do when he woke up late in the night. For now all he needed was rest. He had gone to bed with the figure of the attendant dangling in his mind.

Hours later the tapping at the door woke him up from a long sleep. Manure and Raster entered. They exchanged greetings and walked to the window of his room. They talked about the beauty of the hotel and its fine view that allowed them to see the broad streets of Tripoli and the traffic on three broad lanes. The city seemed to slope at their feet, creating a concavity that gave each street light an extra brightness.

Their first shared dream was to see how they could develop their beloved Kaibara to the status of Tripoli. They agreed that with the diamonds buried in their country, the accomplishment of such a task should be easy. They talked about how they would move the city of RoMarong City from under the toes of the unkempt foothills and transfer it to the flat lands of Gunli, an area already famous for its international airport. While they were still conversing, there was a knock at the door. Borbor Pain opened it to admit the beautiful bar attendant he had seen early in the night. She was carrying the items that Raster had ordered to eat, drink, and smoke.

Borbor Painn drank wine just like he smoked, occasionally. On this night, he kept thinking about the attendant. Raster warned him to be discreet because Islamic laws frowned on extra marital affairs and meted out serious consequences to violators, even as the environment looked secular.

"I had begun to hint to you about our organization, Corporal," said Raster, breaking off the sexual banter. He sipped from his glass and remained silent for a moment. "Now we all are seriously in business and want to keep it so. I have followed your struggle for political justice for some time now, and I believe you found yourself in those prison rags as a result of the frustrations caused by the dictators in our country."

"That was his monkeyish way of protesting," said Manure. "We all have the monkey in us."

Borbor Pain sipped from his glass again and wondered what Raster would have said if he had seen him in tatters under the cotton tree.

"With all my education and my past achievements, I have myself been to Dembapa Prison," said Manure. "Under the first president, who tried everything he could to frustrate me after I opposed his policies."

Raster lit a cigarette and handed one over to Borbor Pain. Macknoon had offered him the same brand before. He wondered if it were the only brand the Libyans had.

"As an activist," said Raster, "I have been fighting for political change within and without Kaibara all my life.

It took us ten years to set up this organization, traveling from continent to continent until we got the support we wanted. Today with our headquarters set in Libya, we are thankful to God for how far he has taken us in this struggle."

Borbor Pain felt the wine mixing with his dreams. He felt old pages flipping in the library of his heart. For a moment his mind raced to the two military coups he had co-staged, the beatings at Dembapa Prison he had received, the daily line-ups in cuffs along the streets of RoMarong City to attend long trials, the façade in the newspapers, the threats of execution, and the frustration of losing his woman when he needed her most.

"All over the world we have governments, statesmen, human rights activists, power brokers, and intellectuals who support our cause. We have held conferences, symposiums, and rallies in different parts of the world to campaign for pressure to be applied to the government to allow political pluralism. While we continue to wait for these responses to be made, we have come up with many ideas of how we, as Kaibarans, will build up pressure at home to get the government to listen to us. It is for one of these measures that Dr. Manure and I have welcomed you with open arms. We feel you are a God-sent person."

Borbor Pain's heart pounded in excitement. He raised his glass but returned it to the table without drinking. He shifted his eyes to look at the ever-flowing traffic. He wondered if Tripoli was a city that went to sleep.

Before coming to Tripoli, he had thought that all of North Africa was just desert and camels.

"Corporal, I personally identified you and recommended you to Raster," said Manure. He cleared his throat, breaking in on the thoughts of Borbor Pain. "As soon as you began to speak at the Jepehun rally, I noticed the fire in you. And I told Raster at once. You see, we have come a long way in the struggle. All of us—you, me, Raster, and so on."

Borbor Pain noticed Manure's pitch becoming irregular. He certainly was drinking his share of the booze. The blue ray of the bulb hanging overhead mapped out the lines on his wrinkled face. He sure was long in the struggle, he agreed.

"I have seen days in government and out of it. I am aware of the many strides we could have made but for the greed and corruption of the governments of today and yesterday. Why should we not build a city like Tripoli with all its road networks and streetlights? Why should we not erect five star hotels like this one all over Kaibara? The answer is— the government is greedy and corrupt."

Borbor Pain remembered that Manure was a government minister when he and others staged the first coup. He felt like asking him but thought his question might be embarrassing at that moment. However, he remembered him as the minister who had fallen out with government over the allegation that he, Manure, had stealthily diverted an entire government shipment of fertilizers from Europe to an undisclosed West African country where he had sold it. Returning home, Manure was said to have distributed rotten seeds to members of the National Farmers' Cooperation, telling them there was fertilizer in each seed.

Raster knew when to cut in. "The latest now, Corporal, is that this city where you are currently sitting, has offered to train our soldiers, to make them ready for battle. We are not preaching violence; we only want to build a standing army that will back the revolution."

Borbor Pain exhaled long and slowly. Why were other people realizing his dream? He knew war was the only solution for a ruthless regime. There were times when under the cotton tree, he had thought, and sometimes had even had visions of an army he wanted to stand against the government.

"The point is, Corporal," Manure added, "We don't want the international community to see us as violent revolutionaries. They will be quick to call us terrorists. Even though we have resolved that we need an army on hold…"

Borbor Pain interrupted before Manure could finish his sentence, "Let us say an army on the front line to help, in case!"

"We hope not, Corporal. We hope we don't have to be pushed to that point. You are right though. Our aim for the establishment of an army is similar to that of the ANC in South Africa. Only we hope that we will not have to use ours."

"The politicians are senseless and worthless," Borbor Pain said. "Don't expect them to walk off and leave their seats for you to fill? We have to fight them with the power of Winston Churchill and the stubbornness

of Nelson Mandela. I think our course is as noble as
that of Mandela. No one is going to brand us violent
when the cause is noble. Why do you think that with all
that army of the ANC causing terror then in South
Africa, Mandela was awarded the Nobel Peace Prize?
The cause my friends! It is the cause!"

"I admire your fire, Corporal," said Manure. "We
need many like you to burn the hell out of that bunch
of crooks in RoMarong City."

Raster emptied his glass and refilled it. He lit a new
cigarette and pulled in a long drag.

"Corporal, your military background may not be
impressive—what I mean is that you may only be a
corporal—yet you are worth five generals," Manure
paused to reach for his wine. "We have this offer to
make you. We want you to head and control the
revolutionary force we are trying to put in place!"

Borbor Pain felt a rush of blood down his spine, and
an instant pleasure settled in his eyes. "I am flattered by
this honor," he replied.

"To equal yourself to the task, you are free to assume
the title of General.

"No!" Borbor Pain protested. "That will ring too
ambitious. I will remain a corporal."

"Well, what a modest man. I am impressed," Manure
gasped.

"Greatly impressed, Corporal greatly impressed."
Raster said.

Before leaving Tripoli, Borbor Pain was approved to serve as the commander of the military wing in the movement by a council of Kaibarans and their foreign financiers at a closed-door meeting. He was moved to see so many important people who until then had communicated to him only through the words of Manure and Raster.

The team spent three weeks in Libya before moving to South Africa where they held talks with former guerilla fighters. After a lengthy meeting in which it secured the services of a mercenary company, Borbor Pain got his chance to sign an agreement as commander. The team flew to London where they held meetings with Kaibaran exiles and then on to the Ukraine where they inspected arms and negotiated prices. Next they returned to Libya to welcome and train fifteen-hundred Kaibaran youth stolen from college campuses and ghettos on the pretext that they were going to Libya on international scholarships.

9

On a crowded evening in Jepehun, after becoming the military commander, Grabo gave the signal for Borbor Pain to begin his speech to the beleaguered village audience. The sun was sympathetic to him. Occasionally it hid behind the thick wool of clouds, as if to show mercy to the poor folks. Grabo had been one of those who had trained in Libya on the recommendation of Borbor Pain. They both had trained side by side. Borbor Pain had had to put up with Grabo's frustration over his family by changing his approach from comfort to reprimand and then to comfort again before Grabo's mind eased.

Two microphones stood before Borbor Pain. "Let me greet you all in the name of *my* revolution. I come to you as a countryman who believes there are many questions in our lives that need answering. And unlike many others, who sit in their comforts in RoMarong City dictating what is good and bad for us, we are here identifying with your problems. In other words, we as good people are here today discussing the bad things in our bad politicians sitting in RoMarong City interpreting our bad as good!"

The crowd erupted in applause that continued for a long spell before Borbor Pain stretched out his hands indicating quiet.

"'Every land is a holy ground.' Is that not what God said to Moses in the Bible?"

The crowd loudly agreed.

"Then, Kaibara is part of God's holiness," Borbor Pain proclaimed. "This ground on which you now stand is a holy ground, and it is this holiness that politicians in RoMarong City are destroying for you and me. What does the Koran say? Does it not advise Muslims, and indeed all good people, to rise and fight if unbelievers seek to destroy their holiness?"

The crowd murmured in agreement. One or two voices commented on Borbor Pain's understanding of the two Books.

"My message therefore is for both Christians and Muslims. Government is supposed to be for the holiness of God, but now we have pagans, kaffirs, defiling everything in RoMarong City. They are sitting in government to pressure us, sitting on it to keep us down, to make us poor, to steal from us, to make us beggars, and to move us to madness!"

His words moved the crowd close to madness. The applause burst out like a thunderstorm. Many in the crowd raised their fists in the air. "Why did it take so long for someone like this to come to our aid?" someone asked.

"You know," said another, "God has stipulated times for his prophets to appear to save the weak and the poor."

"The man speaks like an angel," said a third. "You can almost see fire spitting from his mouth."

"Whoever said the man is an angel?" said the first. "Angels are not what we want to teach those pot-bellied good-for-nothing folks down RoMarong City a lesson. Can't you see the man is the finest devil ever to walk the earth? Who needs an angel to cross our path? Don't we already have many of them behind bars? With these mighty men around him, who could raise an arm against him?"

"And to make matters worse for the government," said a small boy, "most of these fighters are defected soldiers from the national army."

The boy's mother who stood by him strongly hushed him, "Hold your tongue! This is not for you to say, boy. Were you to be asked how you knew, what would you say?"

The mother looked about her to see whether anyone had heard the comment of her son. But no one was paying attention. However, in fear, she grabbed his son's hand and relocated.

The noise died down. Borbor Pain was again talking into the microphone. His voice carried passed the crowd and echoed in the woods. His security gave their backs to him; they were concerned though with the unending bush paths. They had to be vigilant in the event that anyone, as Borbor Pain had warned, either from within or without, wanted to create a scene. Such a person must be dealt with swiftly, according to his orders.

The fighters had been with him long enough now to know when he meant an order to be carried out. The fighters had been taught to talk very little even to each other. Borbor Pain had always told them that the country's military had failed because it lacked discipline and that there were so many chains of command that the soldiers were confused about which orders to act on.

With them, only Borbor Pain's voice gave the command. He gave the order to advance or to retreat, to pull or to draw, to make camp or to move, to rise or to fall. He had warned them about his heart, that it was not made of blood and flesh, and that it did not accommodate sorrow. It only had one big rock in the center that had been placed there for a purpose.

However, when it came to providing his men with what they needed, his hard-rock heart softened. He gave them everything—he himself wanted nothing. He gave them food in abundance. He made sure they had every kind of narcotic, which he told them were morale boosters. He even arranged for women to be available for them. His fighters had come to consider him a workable combination of good and evil. He himself had told them once that he had a bittersweet personality. Everything he did or said proved his depiction quite accurate.

As he spoke, he aroused the crowd with his sarcastic description of what he called "the enemy of the people, the enemy within." He looked around him and was satisfied that he had impressed them greatly. He could see joy in the faces of the elderly and flickers of excitement in the young. As he concluded his talk, he looked around to examine the fine young men and women who would soon sign up for the revolution. He had an instinct about such things.

"Young men and women of this ancient town of warriors, were your fathers and mothers who stood their ground to protect this town here today, they would have sounded their trumpets, they would have fastened their calicos, they would have sharpened their swords, they would have tabled their concerns under the image of their gods in the sacred shrines where the spirits of their own dead now rest, and they would have leaped into action to defend their land which they truly meant to protect for you."

A certain spirit hovered above the crowd and draped them in fear. It was as if in response, the spirits of the dead had really appeared and were taking control of everything around them. Some even confessed they felt the spirits in their bones urging them to rise.

Borbor Pain took one deep breath, shut his eyes, and murmured something to himself. He grasped the microphone from its stand and waved it above his head three times before replacing it. He then opened his eyes and asked the crowd to observe a minute's silence for their dead.

One heard the resonance of war as the crowd said, "Amen!"

"Our elders say if someone sends a shower on you, bathe yourself. Kaibara surely belongs to us all. If you look around, you will see young men and women with guns in their hands doing exactly what your ancestors did a long time ago and what they would do today were they here. My message is simple. I have only this one time to pass through your town. There would be many among your children, who would say, 'I wish I had been born then,' or 'I wish I had been in that crowd when the Corporal and his freedom fighters came passing by. I would have abandoned everything I had and followed him.'

"Tomorrow when our history shall be written in thick books, how would we want to be remembered? Among those who were left behind in the crowd? Or among those who leaped like tigers and roared like lions?"

About thirty men, moved by the speech, clamored in the crowd, "Sign me up!" Soon the crowd became restless. Grabo went forward and tried to calm and direct them to where they should sign up. Surging in that direction, the crowd burst into a war song.

The woman who had shouted at her son to keep quiet lost grip of him as the boy dashed to sign up. The mother rushed after him and seized him by the hem of his shirt. A struggle ensued, but the boy escaped leaving behind his mother and his shirt.

Nervous, the woman then forced her way into the thick of the rowdy crowd, pulling and pushing until she found herself standing before a smiling Borbor Pain.

She hesitated. Her eyes were swollen with tears as she cupped her hands under her chin and knelt before him.

"You must help me, Master. You must help me," she said crying.

"What may I do for you, woman?" Borbor Pain asked.

"My son, my son! He has gone to sign up with the others, and he is too young to go. He is only thirteen. Stop him please before he behaves foolishly."

"Woman, whom do people say that I am?" Borbor Pain enquired.

The woman, confused, just stared at him.

"Pick yourself up from the ground, woman. The boy is a child of the revolution. He has only been moved by his thirteen years of bitterness and only he can change his own situation."

"But he is only a boy, and besides his father will return this evening from Bunumbu where he went to trade. Please, please, Master," the woman was crying bitterly.

"Woman, stop being foolish! Not even God can change the boy's mind." Borbor Pain turned and began to walk away. He felt someone pulling him from the back. He quickly turned to face Raster who had just arrived to witness the scene between the woman and him.

"Why don't we allow the mother to have her son back?" Raster brought the boy from behind him and guided him toward his mother.

Borbor Pain's face hardened. Quickly seizing the boy, he pulled him back and ordered him to rejoin the registration line. Raster was shocked by Borbor Pain's behavior. He first turned to the woman who opened her mouth in awe. Then he faced Borbor Pain again.

"Corporal, we cannot use a child to fight a war," he said angrily. "And besides, we have not declared any war yet! This will be seen as an act of child abuse."

"Child abuse! Yes, anyone can fight a war. Was it child abuse when God allowed David to fight Goliath? And for your information, I already declared a war in that white man's machine." He pointed at the BBC reporter.

Raster turned to look in the direction of the reporter who had been attracted by the standoff. About a year earlier, Raster had feared that Borbor Pain was misdirecting the revolution and was acting rather arrogantly. Since then he had warned him many times and had reminded him that it was only the stubbornness of the government that had led them to think about a small fighting group, but there was no intention for the movement to provoke a war.

"Corporal, I order you to call off this registration right now! You have no right to declare a war," Raster said.

Borbor Pain faced him, and almost whispered. "I will not allow you to disrupt this meeting just because you want to dictate who does what!" meaning that he would not allow Raster to humiliate him before a people who now considered him a god.

"Corporal, do you know how much damage your action will be doing to the revolution? We are just coming from a council meeting and—"

"Oh, don't tell me anything about a council meeting! I am having my own meeting here," Borbor Pain sneered

130

"Don't forget that you have superiors above you," Raster said.

His words fell on Borbor Pain like a hammer. "Certainly, not you! On this ground only my men and I make decisions. And for your information, for any revolution to succeed, everyone has to be equal to each other. Here, my men and I are equal to each other. Not like it is with you and your so-called council that mimics the government you oppose, only to lord it over these poor people again.

Siding with Borbor Pain, the crowd burst into laughter.

"I can't believe this is happening. I think you are a curse to this organization. I should have known it before!" Raster yelled, moving toward the registration line. "I now believe you are actually mad!"

"Soldier!" Borbor Pain called, growling like a lion in the woods.

An armed guard mechanically responded and turned to face Borbor Pain.

"Arrest that man now!" he pointed to Raster.

Raster heard the order and immediately felt the powerful arms of the soldier upon him. The soldier swung him by the neck and gathered his hands behind. He handcuffed Raster and pushed him toward Borbor Pain.

Raster struggled to free himself. "Are you mad, soldier? You should be listening to me and not him! Look here! Let me go! Let me go!"

Borbor Pain leaned in on Raster, pushing his face almost to the point of touching. He whispered in a

131

heavy breath, "You are nothing but a hindrance on my path. Get thee behind me, Satan! Have you heard that verse before?"

Raster remained quiet. He saw the fire in the corporal's eyes.

"Kill him!" Borbor Pain instructed another soldier while still eying Raster.

Shocked, the soldier stepped backward. He looked with fear into the red eyes of Borbor Pain.

Sensing the reality of the command Raster began to tremble. "What are you doing? You can't do this to me! We can talk it over. Go ahead and register the boy if you like!"

"Kill him I say! Shoot him!" Borbor Pain growled.

At that moment it was as if he heard someone whispering in his ear that if he himself were to kill Raster, he would secure himself immense respect from the villagers. His vision showed him the image of a victorious warrior. He heard a distant jubilation. The sound of a trumpet filled the air. He had hated Raster's eagerness. He always hated to see eagerness in people who wanted to outshine him, just as he had hated his eager platoon mates who had acted with such cowardliness against his advice and had betrayed his two military coups.

The guard cocked his gun. Borbor Pain stopped him. Removing his berretta and raising it between himself and Raster in the stillness of the woods, he pulled the trigger.

"You are now a footnote, Raster," he said, immensely pleased with himself.

132

It was the winter of my discontent, and the narrator was already aware that I feared the harsh weather of New York. He allowed me to return to my home of exile.

10

The winter of 1997 was biting in NYC. I met with my three "learners," for lack of a proper term, twice a week, and two hours a day. I allowed them to regulate the schedule, since I was retired and without a regular engagement. The classes were informal; however, I was expected to forward a monthly report of their progress. The class was made up of a married couple from Mexico and an unmarried Ukrainian man.

With the New York City Literacy Service, it was customary for the first two classes to be conducted in the headquarters of the organization for supervision's sake. Afterward, classes could be held anywhere as long as the locations were within the state and were agreeable to by everyone.

The Mexican lady was young, the men in their mid-sixties, so many years younger than me. However, I carried myself like a fifty-something year-old and sometimes felt even younger. That was exactly what the Mexican lady said aloud after I announced my age. I had no weight problem and only few complaints of fatigue. I owed it all to my daughter who had always seen to it that I exercised at least every weekend. During the past years of living alone, I had been very diligent with my push-ups. Yolanda had also taught me to keep my eyes open to men's fashions. I had convinced myself that early retirement would help me keep my spirit alive until my planned return to Kaibara, the latter of which Yolanda wasn't interested in at all.

The classes were always lively, and my learners looked forward to them. After a short while during which the teacher and learners formed friendships, we became a small family and felt at ease in discussing personal issues in our small meetings. Like me, the learners had sought political asylum in America, and, as the Mexican lady put it, they jumped directly from the frying pan into the fire. Fernando, her husband, told us that he had exposed a drug cartel involving untouchable Mexican politicians. His actions had cost him his two children. He said the sheriff in his small town of Durango had promised him government protection, but on the night of the assault, it was the sheriff himself whom he saw smashing into his door, while the deputy seized his two children and fled with them into the night. Three men walked into his bedroom like shadows brandishing their naked bodies ready to rape his wife. With all of his might, he had tightened his grip around her, and together they had leaped through a window.

His wife only nodded with a painful smile, but she had said little beyond announcing her name, which I found musically interesting: *Barabara*.

Her husband was quick to speak up. "Eh, Bar – she name Barbara," he said. "Spanish is be Barabara." His pronunciation somehow sounded funny to me, but I laughed only a little and suppressed the rest in my belly.

Chernobyl, the Ukrainian, a former soldier with a face as vacant as a desert, told us only that he had defected from his country's military force. In anticipation that he had more to say, we remained silent; however, he only raised his head, giggled, and said something in Ukrainian that none of us understood. The only word I caught was *Africa* but I didn't know in what context he had used it. By this disposition, it crossed my mind that Chernobyl's relationship with his country's army hadn't etiolated even if the military didn't think of him anymore. Added to that impression, I had the feeling that the ex-soldier was holding something back.

Owing to my spiritual attachment to the program and my penchant for conversation, I soon asked them to share their experiences in oral English. In this way, I was privileged to learn more about their countries.

When the class had first begun, it was difficult for us all. None of the learners knew more than five words of English, including general greetings. I had to put up with their one liner expressions whenever the messages seemed difficult to get across. Actually, all they needed was working English. They were simple and humble immigrants who were barely scraping the hard surface of survival, and they didn't hide the truth that they were comfortable with the menial jobs America had to offer them. From the day I told them I was a trained attorney, they looked upon me with the utmost respect.

On one evening, we met at Chernobyl's one-room apartment. Chernobyl lived alone, yet one would think his apartment was a playground for kids. Everything was unkempt. Regardless of the threatening winter, he didn't keep a heater; at least, none was on to keep the class warm. A biological odor hung in the room. It was as disheveled as his hair.

Chernobyl never wore a bright face. Dark glasses and dark clothes hid his face even when he was not in the open. Standing close to him, we could feel his asthmatic breath and heard a constant clicking sound from inside his mouth. He frequently fidgeted with his nose as though he wished it had filled his face so he could breathe freely. His eyes always peered about as if he were searching for a tiny article on the ground. He spoke very little, with even less possibility of being understood. During classes, he mechanically reached for a cigarette but put it away as though the others had warned him against smoking.

On that particular day, after the class ended, he dashed to his fridge and came hopping back with a bottle of the strongest liquor in town. Barbara and I declined the offer and requested water instead. Chernobyl and Fernando finished the bottle between exchanging unintelligible Ukrainian and Mexican jokes with unreliable English as the bridge. The expression *Africa* and *Kaibara* kept coming from his mouth. At once I concluded that I was being gossiped. I expected such sentiments to exist, given that I was the first black person all three of them had ever come closest to in America. However, the feeling that Chernobyl was holding back something returned to me over and over.

Fernando was five feet, six inches tall, but he stood a little shorter because of a stoop. His nose reminded me of a train passing through a tunnel. He talked too much and seemed to utter his words without thinking them through, so he frequently confused Spanish with English words.

His wife, Barbara, conducted herself with coyness and seemed to express herself better when rolling back her long hair with her left hand and tucking the excess hair into a bob with her right. Even though she towered over her husband, she gathered herself under him like a young cub. Her eyes peered at him from behind her glasses, which she took off him only to look into a book. Very soon, the two men were snoring, leaving me and Barbara with little between us to keep the conversation rolling.

On my way home, I tuned on my car radio just in time to catch the news of the war in my beloved Kaibara. The rebels had engaged government forces in a 36-hour battle, the newscaster said. Government sources reported that for lack of timely backup from the provincial town of Kameni from which, due to lack of sufficient vehicles, the military had had to make a tactical withdrawal. The withdrawal of the government troops provided an opportunity for the guerrilla fighters to advance further east, killing an unbelievable number of civilians and capturing a thousand others to be

138

paraded before them as human shields. The rebels had seized the country's diamond province, Nokoh. This latest victory for the rebels split Kaibara in half, with the economic half under the control of the rebels.

The news of the capture of Nokoh was followed by a short commentary from a former British High Commissioner to Kaibara. He was quick to say the war was as a result of a diamond conflict. I had heard this trash many times before and had been angry at the world for believing it. While I agreed that diamonds had heavily funded the war, I didn't agree that a conflict about diamonds had ignited the war. Diamonds might have helped prolonged the war, but the real cause of the Kaibara war had nothing to do with them. It was crystal clear to anyone who had followed Kaibara's political history that the war was as a result of injustices and lack of a decent and ethical political leadership

I felt that the western media (influenced by their own history of post-industrial corruption over minerals in the belly of their own earth) had hastily and wrongly envisioned greed in my country, whose population (until the war broke out) had no spiritual connection to its diamonds. I feared that this assumption had left the real culprits unpublished in newspapers and un-discussed in the news. They should have known that the Kaibara conflict had its history in the sociopolitical injustices flagrantly meted out against defenseless Kaibarans like myself following the premature and haphazard exit of the British colonialists.

A sharp wobbling noise under my car brought me out of my reverie. I had been too engrossed in the news to notice it at first. I was in the middle of the street, in the middle of a New York City street with a dozen other vehicles on my trail. I attempted to move to the right. The car kicked forcefully as though the tires had gone flat. I turned the wheel in the other direction. Fortunately, I was able to pull off to the side where the engine came to an abrupt stop with a loud clanging. I tried to restart it, but couldn't. I stepped out and discovered my alternator on the ground. My battery was dead, and the fan belt had broken. Without much ado, I dialed my tow company from my cell phone as I began to redirect the traffic behind me. New York was busy, but that didn't stop two youths in a dirty car that heaved heavy, staccato rap beats from poking their heads out to size me up. A nearby homeless man offered me a place in his box while laughing like someone choking under water. A woman confused by the uncaring crowd thought it would be good for me to abandon my car, and indeed the world, forever and find respite in her embrace.

I rarely used cabs. When I didn't use my car, I caught the bus, which was five times cheaper than a taxi, but after the break down that evening, I had needed to return home urgently to meet the tow-company that was taking my car to my apartment. However, this time, I had no choice. I hailed a taxicab and told the driver my address in as few words as possible. The driver seemed to be a professional with an accurate knowledge of New York, for he didn't request any further information. I saw him readjusting his meter as we drove off. Luckily for me, his radio was tuned to the station mine had been in my car. Kaibara again came on the news, but it was mostly a repeat of the earlier news. I rested my head on the back of the seat and left behind me a New York of broken cars, tainted youth, a collapsed adult, and a city mermaid starved for sex and cash.

Suddenly I sat up, seized by an additional piece of news. Rebels under the warlord fighting in the neighboring country had been seen marching into Kaibara like Neanderthal guerrillas to support the rebels there in their bid to oust the government. The neighboring warlord was making real his threat to punish Kaibara for allowing the newly formed ECOWAS Monitoring Group, or ECOMOG (a combination of West African forces put together by the member countries of the regional organization Economic Community of West African States, or (ECOWAS), settle in that country to sabotage his rebellion.

Throughout the cab ride, the driver hadn't spoken a word. I noticed that he hadn't stopped nodding his head and sucking his teeth since I boarded his taxi. I looked at his ears to see if he was wearing headphones and listening to music, for it had become fashionable for taxi drivers to carry Walkman devices on them as they drove around New York. But he had no headphones.

The broadcast on Kaibara was unusually long with interviews done with a spokesman of the government of the neighboring country, a Kaibaran human rights activist, and the commander of ECOMOG.

141

"That is a stupid thing!"

I was shocked to hear the driver speak, but I didn't let his comment pass unchallenged.

"I beg your pardon," I said.

Mechanically, he swept a look back at me and giggled, "Oh, no, no. I was just talking to myself. Excuse my— I'm sorry—was I that loud?"

I felt at ease and allowed myself a smile. "Oh, okay. I myself do the same every so often when my mind is heavy, you know." I laughed. I added to myself that the mind being a terrible thing could move the cabman to dump his car in some godforsaken pit.

The driver looked like someone who needed pity. He had long since returned to his nodding silence and teeth sucking. I could hear the full beat of the engine. The day began cold and gloomy and was expected to end in like manner. I began to imagine the worse for myself. Had I been in Kaibara when the war started, considering that I was with the engineers of the rotten system, I would have suffered its fate.

"You heard me grumbling to myself, eh?" said the driver. "It's just that the news is about my country. A civil war has been going on in my small country, Kaibara, which is in West Africa. And hearing all this…" he shook his head. "It makes me sick. You can see why I cursed in my breath."

It wasn't that I didn't expect to find a Kaibaran that evening on the streets of New York, after all there were also unruly hip hop youths, a beggar and a woman starving for sex; but I was unprepared for the bittersweet effect of suddenly discovering someone with a heart that had already been struck by enough arrows of western misconceptions paraded in the media regarding the Kaibara war.

"You are a Kaibaran? So am I, brother! This is so— my brother—something which could have been prevented," I groaned.

"Are you too a Kaibaran?" the driver turned to look at me as he paused at a red light. His words were not a question.

"What a sick Kaibaran I am," I sighed.

"A small world this is," he turned again to look at me, sucking his teeth.

"A sick Kaibaran, that I am," I repeated.

"Sick? Could there be any one more frustrated than I am?" It was meant to be rhetorical.

"I guess every one of us Kaibarans is as sick as the other no matter where we find ourselves," I said, cautious about making known my position because I had met Kaibarans who had expressed unflinching support for one side to the point of violence.

"That good for nothing zealot. Whoever told him that war is what we want in our country, to unseat an equally good for nothing government?" he thundered.

I always expressed my anger beginning with the era of the president I had served, and I would nurture it all the way to the battle between the forces of the rebels and the current government. I ended up apportioning more blames to the government side and castigating the international community for siding with the government against the ordinary citizens and the demands of the rebels. I thought the war a necessary evil, although at the same time, I knew the rebellion was in the wrong hands. But what do you do with a leadership that was muzzling the voice and freedom of its citizens? Borbor Pain was to me a necessary evil. I quickly realized the taxi driver's position as being a rather peripheral one, casting blames on the fight-back position of the rebels. I thought it was time to begin to make a case for Borbor Pain and his rebellion.

"Whoever gave birth to that lion? All he is thirsty for is blood," the cabbie said. "Do you think the rebel leader is an average Kaibaran? He is the most heartless rebel leader plying the forests of Africa. Just think about the many amputees that have been made out of Kaibarans, eh? The rebel leader and his band of men are cannibals. They are cannibals! Otherwise, what would anyone want to do with human limbs?"

He reduced the volume of his radio because the news had shifted to some other war in some other country.

"Who do they want to rule after the war?" he asked, making a left turn. "After they have maimed everyone and killed those they have to kill and buried the elders before their time, what nation are we left with?"

I was tempted to say, "A nation of shadows." That was a line from one of my daughter's verses written about racism.

"I don't really understand the very government that would not want to open the public spaces for more people to participate," I began my statement challenging that of the driver.

"My brother, nobody will understand people like the rebels. I tell you those guys are not your average Kaibarans."

Although I sensed that we didn't look at the war from the same angle, whereas I supported a rebellion and he angry with the rebels' bloody trail, yet we both criticized the western media for the manner in which it was reporting the war. We became bitter brothers inside his taxicab that winter evening in New York.

"It is the western world that is fueling the war," said the driver. "How else do you think the rebels would obtain ammunition to maintain a war that long? You remember Persia? You remember Angola? You just wait and see how their interest would turn around," my new friend said.

"But RoMarong City can afford to sell itself for *cocoa-ebe*," I lamented. It was not always that I came to use a Kaibaran domestic expression like *cocoa-ebe*, which stood for the porridge of cocoa, but with the cabman jumping into Krio, I took the nostalgic leap myself.

The driver sucked his teeth. "And as for Colonel Khadafy, somebody needs to give him a punch for supporting the rebels," he rather threw his fist in the air as if it was the expected punch itself.

One theory that circulated long before the war broke out was that, as farfetched as it sounded, the origin of the Kaibara war could be traced to a political conflict that occurred long ago between the Kaibaran president and the Libyan Colonel, Mommar Khadafy (It was not just a quarrel between the Libyan leader and our president, it was one that involved several sub-Saharan countries who sided America during the cold war with the then USSR). I was a senior government official at the time closely linked to the issue; it was an event that took place long before anyone thought of a war; however, I waited the cabman to develop the point. Like many others I had heard mentioning the war, he didn't know the depth of it. Moreover, I had already come too close to my destination to broach the topic. But I felt I needed to serve as the devil, Borbor Pain's advocate:

"Let me ask you a question," I said to the driver, "Is it all the time that someone goes into another's house and attack one for the way one is living in it?"

The driver took a look at me in his front mirror as if I was not there all this time. "No, of course not," he said looking at me again.

"Suppose we also look at the terrible misdeeds of the government of Kaibara, down the lane of history, the mayhems they have caused families, towns and other people outside their own thinking, and how that could have pushed people to the wall to fight back?"

"Everyone must have freedom like the one we are enjoying here in America. Like you and I moving freely about and people talking about things freely," he said.

"Well, imagine that you and I can achieve all that freedom here in America but cannot achieve it back home. As a matter of fact we are here because we are searching for that freedom."

"I can understand where you are going with this. And I have family in Kaibara who tell me they are in a police

146

state. They cannot say anything without watching left and right," the cabbie said.

"I tell you my brother, the rebels might have angered you, but it is always courageous to fight back to achieve one's freedom. Most of that destruction you talk about might have been perpetrated by the government to gain national and international sympathy," I said.

For a short spell, I could see the cabbie peering through into the length of the avenue we were on. He eventually sucked his teeth. "Phew! Phew!" was all he said.

When we arrived in front of my apartment, I told him the conversation was good but incomplete. I liked the way we handled the issue. There were one or two matters we certainly had not fully handled, but we honestly agreed on how frustrated both of us were about events in Kaibara.

He hit the meter of the car, and it stopped.

"How much ah owe you-o?" I asked as I stepped out the taxi.

"A lot; you owe a lot to our people back home. As for the ride, consider it on me for that brilliant analysis of yours," he said, winking his left eye in a friendly manner.

"No, no. It doesn't have to be like that. While I appreciate your appreciating me, I have to pay. This is New York, and your pot's got to boil."

"Here is my name and telephone contact," he said taking out a business card and handing it to me. "This is where my pot boils whenever you have time to hang around." He laughed and stepped on the gas.

147

I followed the cab with my eyes as it pulled away. Returning my fare along with his contact information, to my pocket, I whispered, "Thanks all the same."

11

The narrator invited me to sail with him on a boat. Although the boat was moving away from land, yet I had no clue where we were headed. It seemed to me that he had an idea of where we were headed and so I decided to sit and take the ride with him:

Just before killing Manure Gallon in the diamond heartland of Nokoh, Borbor Pain had said to him, "So that you too, resting in perpetual peace shall know that this is not just a rebellion, but the rebellion of the indefatigable Corporal."

His blade had come down on Gallon like a butcher's clever. It struck the soft flesh of his shoulder and sank into the very joint, causing the arm to hang and opening a passage to the heart. Borbor Pain was not in a hurry. He withdrew the knife and paused to watch Manure's blood gush, to the ground. Grabo continued to hold the other hand as was commanded. He turned him around. Assisted in this way by Grabo, Borbor Pain had the leisure to strike in a calm and calculated manner. He broke him and then motioned for Grabo to let him go. Manure's upper body pitched to the ground supported by his dying hands. His legs spread wide apart inside the oversized jeans he always wore to visit Borbor Pain in the battlefront. He assumed the posture of an unfinished artwork.

Borbor Pain could not understand why a man broken to the last bones would still beg for mercy. Perhaps his last hopes were in his eyes after which he would give up. In response, Borbor Pain reached for them and plucked them out. With one groan, Manure writhed in a pool of his own blood. He was still begging for mercy!

"Finish him off!" Borbor Pain ordered, turning away from the macabre sight. He heard the blast of Superman's gun and there was a total silence.

Superman strutted about the corpse with pride. He went up to Grabo to ask him what to do with the body. It was Borbor Pain's idea that for anything any of his fighters wanted to do, Grabo must give the okay, but Grabo, as always, was disturbed by the horrible demise of Manure so he shut his eyes to the sight of him.

Superman loved the fun when it came to "disappearing" someone. That was how they referred to killing. Superman was an original revolutionary, meaning he was a recruit of the Dembapa Prison. He considered himself third in command in the battlefield.

Sometimes he even thought of himself as the second in command. Somehow he felt Grabo didn't merit the second position. He had the mind of an angel, Superman would say. Whereas Borbor Pain had handpicked Grabo for the second in command, Superman had worked his way right up to the third. He would do everything to promote himself. Years after that dramatic rescue from Dembapa Prison, he knew he had discovered a game that he would love.

Manure Gallon would have dismissed any seer who would ever have told him his life was going to end the way it did. As the executive director of the organization, Manure Gallon least expected that Borbor Pain, a mere field commander, would be the one to plan his death. He knew he had had a rivalry that had competed with him for the leadership of the organization. But Borbor Pain? He had always believed that the man was mad and had a deep-rooted bitterness toward the politicians in RoMarong City. It was for this reason, in fact, that Manure had recommended his selection to command the fighting wing of the organization.

"But we want to be sure that he will not compete with us for the leadership of the party once we are in RoMarong City," Raster had cautioned.

"Talk of another thing," Manure had cackled. "He doesn't have the kind of education and clout to lead a country."

Unfortunately, they had failed to see that Dracula had once sunk his teeth into Borbor Pain's neck and that his

151

blood was contaminated in such a way that he was desperate for the blood of others, especially of those he found contesting with him. From the moment Borbor Pain heard Manure and Raster speaking, he knew he didn't like them. As they opened their mouths to speak he saw the arrogance of the educated Kaibarans who sat in the nation's university theorizing the failure of state governance and rising to power themselves, only to became more corrupt and despotic. He had seen too many like them to trust anyone.

With all his education, Manure didn't see the signal from Raster's death. Maybe he was too occupied with his own ambition of attaining power and becoming rich at the same time. He was always conscious of his age and knew unless he was aggressive enough he would probably not fulfill his dream of ruling Kaibara and becoming rich before he died.

He had come to the leadership of the organization after making a name for himself in politics.

One evening, Borbor Pain had radioed him to say Raster had had a scuffle with one of the child-combatants who were under the influence of drugs. The boy, not realizing who Raster was, had opened fire and killed him with six bullets to his belly. Manure had felt grief over the loss of Raster, but inside he knew that by Raster's death the organization was bound to become his personal property.

So instead of replacing Raster with some other person, he took to visiting the battlefront himself. Many at times, dressed in a soldier's fatigues he had tested and fired a gun at imaginary enemies. Borbor Pain even gave him a gun to carry about in the battlefront in case government troops attacked. However, he never encountered any action during his visits to the front, but after what had happened to Raster, he never went close to the fighters. He entertained them only in the presence of Borbor Pain. Borbor Pain had loved it that way, up to that fatal day in Nokoh.

For the single desire of capturing the diamond heartland of Nokoh, Manure had efficiently monitored the war. He knew it was because of Nokoh that the organization had received major financial support from their partners. They had to capture Nokoh urgently, otherwise their support would be cut off.

"Our chances are great," Borbor Pain had assured Manure, shortly before they seized Nokoh. "Superman has just returned from a village near Nokoh. His sources told him that the town is vulnerable."

"You have to work these guys hard! We haven't got much time to reach RoMarong City," Manure had said. "Get your guys to go in at whatever cost, Corporal. It is very important that we seize Nokoh before the end of the month. What do you think?"

Borbor Pain had nodded calmly. When he spoke, it was on another subject. Looking at the sky he said, "Do you believe it has not rained on us for two months?"

"Get your men to take over Nokoh, and you will have all the rain you want. In the meantime, the town must be taken immediately and by any means necessary."

"The trouble is that we have been having problems with getting willing recruits. We have had to get rough in replacing our fallen men," he said, wanting to determine Manure's moral standing.

"Corporal, you certainly have to do all you can to capture Nokoh immediately. I trust that you know how to get your men. Gag them. Threaten them. Do all you can, but get a replacement. We need Nokoh today. We need Nokoh now! What about your child-soldiers?"

The road to capture Nokoh had been made on the backs of his many rebels. For that was how Borbor Pain defined the death of revolutionaries. He had done everything to impress his rebels. He told them the cause was greater than anyone was, and that whoever fell short of it could be "disappeared," depending on the nature of the crime. Raster had committed irreparable damage for which death was the ultimate penalty.

There was a time when Borbor Pain himself had committed a few crimes by falling short of his infinite standards, but they were those inevitable ones that occurred every now and then. He had however offered them his throat to slit, reminding them of the law being above every one of them, but his trusted men bellowed and rebuked him for his overzealous offer. Grabo had even overheard Superman saying the laws didn't affect Borbor Pain, for he was already a law unto himself. Grabo believed Borbor Pain had always timed his act well, otherwise why didn't he do it when the rebels were under the influence of drugs?

Borbor Pain established the roots of his prime position in the movement after he killed Raster in

Jepehun and shed Manure's blood in the diamond town of Nokoh. For his rebels, nothing had changed. Borbor Pain had always been their leader. Manure and all others who had visited occasionally reminded them of the clean shaved politicians who sat in towering offices behind oversized mahoganies and harsh glinting lenses. It had even been rumored at one time that Manure and Raster were not really part of the organization and had been visiting from the other side to negotiate peace with Borbor Pain.

On the day of his death, Manure had received a radio call from Borbor Pain with the news that Nokoh had fallen into their hands. Manure had screamed aloud and shouted, "Diamonds! Diamonds! These 'Deadmonds' are now 'Wake-monds!'"

"I want to call the BBC on the wire to come here," Borbor Pain had radioed Manure.

"The what? The BBC? And open up our secret to the world?" Manure shouted. "Our partners should be the first to know about this."

"I want the world to know that our course is the people's course, and that we are on our way to the seat of power in RoMarong City."

"*We* want, Corporal. I think the only man to say 'I' in the organization should be Dr. Manure. And for the BBC interview, I don't know. You see the diamonds— vultures will come from everywhere to scavenge on our gains. Let us wait until we solidify our hold on the town," Manure said.

Borbor Pain knew that whenever Manure wanted to humiliate him he called him 'corporal' in a degrading tone. He stood still with his radio to his ear and cursed him under his breath. He hated Manure's guts. "Sir, when are you coming over to give morale support to our boys? They want your pat on their backs. They need it before we set for RoMarong City. "

"You are absolutely right, Corporal. I will be there in three hours. Now if you will let me go…" Manure cut off the line.

"Yes," Borbor Pain breathed out as he killed the line.

Three hours later, Manure was in Nokoh in the company of no one, not even his partners who had waited and waited for the capture of Nokoh. Dressed in white T-shirt and oversized jeans, he walked across the town of his dream. He focused his eyes sharply on the ground, recalling what he had been told as a kid: that on the ground of Nokoh, if one looked carefully, one might find a diamond. Although he no longer believed in the story, he could not help looking carefully as he walked along. He knew that very soon, he would be sending men inside the ground to search for the stone of life!

What he didn't know was that in less than thirty minutes, he would be buried with his head resting on the pillow of the stone of death!

Grabo was to read the charge against Manure, but he had pleaded with Borbor Pain to release him from that task. He didn't have the guts to do it. Superman volunteered to do it. However, instead of reading a charge to Manure, he had intercepted him on the entrance to Borbor Pain's compound, assaulted him, chained his hands to his back, blindfolded him, and stood him before Borbor Pain like a fifty-kilo bag of rice.

Borbor Pain drew a sharp machete from under his chair. A moment later Superman was taking Manure's corpse to be buried in the swamps of the town he had hoped would make him rich and great.

Grabo had swallowed enough of the bitterness of Borbor Pain's ruthless administration. A man who had carved out his life in the bloodless profession of a merchant now bathed his fingers in the blood of innocent victims. The road to capture Nokoh had not been easy for him. There were nights when he dreamed the avenging souls of the dead pursuing him. On those nights, he trembled and cried in his sleep. Other nights, even without dreaming, he had awakened violently out of his sleep to clutch his tortured heart buried inside his chest.

Grabo had used drugs a few times and drank bottles of rum in order to be able to sleep and combat the devil that his conscience had become. He had even shot a few children at close range and licked their blood to ignite in him the permanent fire of Satan. He had stretched virgin girls on streambeds and ordered his men to rape them before him to confront the nudity of sin.

But each time he dove into the bottomless pit, he found himself suspended, far removed from the perfect image of madness characterized by his leader who smiled at the face of pain and wore its garments with ease. Grabo had tried many times to approach suicide with a knife to his throat or a cup of Socratic hemlock in his trembling hand. A man who would commit a flawless suicide must first learn to murder with ease.

If Borbor Pain knew about Grabo's weakness, he never mentioned it. It was clear that at tense moments, he who was supposed to be the second in command was always left out.

The twenty-eight-year-old Superman carried himself in the fashion of his boss and perfected every evil he was asked to carry out. He kept a lot of vigor in him, which Grabo thought was good to regularly combat the devil that was also in him. Superman had very little patience with Grabo and spoke to him only when Borbor Pain forced him to. At times Superman intimidated him. Once Grabo had asked a favor he wanted Superman to do for him.

Superman quickly cut in, "*Ah*, I see you always keep company with angels you can't ward off you. Do you want to hire me to ward them off you? And I mean every word of it."

"Hiring you? What is it for which I would want to hire you?" Grabo asked.

"To redeem you from the angels."

Grabo giggled. "Just how are you going to do that?"

"If you hire me to kill you, I would have saved your weak spirit from many a torment," Superman paused and eyed Grabo with contempt. "You will tell me how you wish to die, but if you trust me I can be as creative as the Corporal."

Grabo gasped, but he was not surprised that Superman would make such a suggestion. He knew that if Superman really wanted to kill him, he could do it and order his body to be thrown away by his personal bodyguards. He remembered Borbor Pain telling him once in confidence that he should select four strong and trusted men to serve him as his bodyguards. It was then that he came to realize that even with that stone of Lucifer inside, Borbor Pain greatly feared his beasts of fighters.

Grabo ignored the suggestion. What did he need a bodyguard for? Just because he, Borbor Pain, had a dozen of them around at all times didn't mean he too should. In fact, he believed that with bodyguards around him, the gadflies of the devil of conscience would torment his soul even more. He would be a potential victim for any rebel's gun. He didn't even carry a gun all the time. There were times when he forgot that he was in the middle of a war and strayed about aimlessly until somebody reminded him that he could one day step into enemy lines.

It was not so much the war that troubled Grabo's mind as did thoughts of his family. Like a dream, so many years had gone by since he last saw his wife in a flash under the central cotton tree in RoMarong City when Borbor Pain had been raving in madness. *Years!* Years added to the ages of his children. Years not being there as a father and a husband, being dead all those years. And—and oh it was coming again. That dreaded vision of—of—

The thought of Nyakoi, motivated by carnal urge, beaming with joy and stretching out—like a sprinter in the hands of a new lover haunted him. Now someone else was in it. There was the bolted door barring him from the face of his children and from his visionless pictures hanging there in his living room. She was there, inside his room that held his belongings, his shoes, his personality, the room that shaped his image, there in the room with another man, his enemy perhaps, his friend, anyone. Perhaps it was someone who owed him money, negotiating a long-term payment that resulted in an acquaintance, an intimacy. Perhaps it was a neighbor who from his verandah had noticed the absence of a husband and a father. Perhaps it was a man who wanted the whole world to know about his conquest over Grabo's wife, someone more attractive than he was, a Casanova, a devil of the night with eyes burning bright with charms, an angel of words and whispers with a personality as vast as the sea. Perhaps it was someone and full of hunger, someone with the appetite of a dog.

In Grabo's thoughts, the man probably had visited Nyakoi in the thick of night, a shadow in the dark. He was a man in a dark dress, and stepping into the darkness and slipping up the back stairs with the quietness of a dark mind to prey. He whispered through the short window that Grabo had constructed for ventilation. He stepped in, careful of the uncompromising children, and yet he announced gifts for them with a wry smile and a mischievous generosity patting Nyakoi's bottom. He probably sat in the easy chair, engaging first in idle conversation, and then complaining about the heat, seeking an excuse to remove his shirt and hanging his stench among Grabo's clean clothes.

He conversed more until Nyakoi showed interest in his lies. Hungry for her, the man quivered like an abandoned child until Nyakoi became sympathetic and turned to him in the darkness of her starvation. She received him—oh God—all the while reflecting on her husband's concern and love. She hesitated and sighed, telling the intruder that it was wrong. They should postpone it for another day, she said, hoping that Grabo would show up one day soon. Hot all over, the man begged her. She resisted harder, seeing God. Irritated, he applied force. She shrieked at first, but laughed afterward—giving hope to the monster. Nyakoi gulped, feeling the hunger from Grabo's absence, letting the devil win. That was it. Nyakoi opened up to receive, and the devil, tense and stern, gathered strength to defame a husband's worth.

Did she lose Grabo in her mind? He had been gone for years, hundreds and hundreds of nights and the tempting figures of the devil groping in the wild. The absences of Grabo's image down the road.

Was his poor Nyakoi alone in a familiar bed with a strange man?

"*Nooo!*" Grabo screamed, coming out of his hallucination while experiencing a violent jolt within.

The gasp had been acidic. He seized a rock under his knapsack, shifted it between his thumb and forefinger and squeezed all his strength into it. In the end he dropped it and soothed the pain inside his fingers. The mind had raced too far into every dirty thought. It was time to act like a man. It was time to die like a man. He was nearly always alone. He hardly had anyone to talk to except when someone needed a supply of ammunition.

It was always Grabo who took the matter to Borbor Pain, but it was Borbor Pain who released every weapon. Borbor Pain had told them that in every country, the president was also the Minister of Defense. Only he had access to all weapons. Actually Grabo had no interest in his ammunition or any of his political schemes. All he cared about all this time was to be in the embrace of Nyakoi and his children.

There were times when he and Bassie, the prison warden who had untied Grabo's shoes at Dembapa Prison, sat long into the night. Bassie had been disillusioned by the blood and gore of the organization and by the failed promises he and others like him in government services had received. He had been tempted to betray his loyalty to the government for a new situation once the organization seized power, but years into the struggle, all he could account for was a transgression against innocent people.

After discovering that they both felt the same way, they confided in each other. The night of Bassie's escape, which Grabo had helped him plan, Bassie had told everything to Grabo. Grabo had written a letter to Nyakoi for Bassie to deliver for him. He had said goodbye to Bassie under their usual meeting place, and the latter had disappeared into the belly of the night with a small pistol hidden in his pants.

Two nights later, Bassie was brought before Borbor Pain whipped and naked. Borbor Pain handed him over to Superman who had just smoked a bag of Mary Jane and was high in the sky. He had told Superman that Bassie was his bag of gift.

Borbor Pain's simple message had been that Bassie must be "disappeared" for breaking the law. Superman must have seen two of his victim, because when he raised his machete to strike him it was the air beside him that he slashed. However a fifth blow hooked Bassie under the chin, forcing him to utter a loud scream. Such a scream was a crime of sabotage capable of exposing the rebels' hiding place. The blade struck a second time, and Bassie lay quietly at his executioner's feet.

Grabo mourned bitterly that night for his friend. Now as Grabo thought of Bassie again, he too resolved to attempt an escape. He had heard of the amnesty the government was granting to any rebel who surrendered. The news had been broadcast twice in the BBC and was already a national anthem in the local radio. Borbor Pain in turn ordered the execution of any of his men who tried to escape, and as many had attempted it were butchered under the watch of a ruthless leader.

The thought of his wife returned regularly to him. The images were specific: the shadowy image of a man, his friend or his enemy, with his wife. It was at a time like this that he appreciated the notion that a thought hurt more than a slap, more than a kick, more than a machete's blow, more than a bullet. A thought lingered for long time. A thought can kill.

He prepared himself. The many visions of his family had mesmerized him. He was going to escape in the same way Bassie had planned to. The night with no astrological kiss engulfed him. And his resolve was such that no night could scare him.

The narrator suddenly stopped narrating. In the ensuring silence, it seemed to me that the ebb and tide of the sea had taken over the narration. I couldn't tell whether by casting his eyes on the sea, the narrator was himself listening to a different kind of story. After a while he turned the boat around and we sailed for the land we had left a long distance behind us.

12

In my apartment, I poured myself a glass of wine and sat to watch the television. I fidgeted with the phone. There were messages waiting for me on the answering machine. One was from Yolanda. She had stopped by on her way to work. She wanted me to call her when I got home. She just wanted to know how I was doing. Her mother was doing fine, she said. Both of them were out last night to visit her mother's doctor.

Doctor? How long has she been seeing a doctor and for what? I wasn't sure what my wife was up to. I was still baffled by her not trying to fill me in on why she walked out of my life.

When I had first arrived in the United States, an American friend of mine had told me he and his wife had divorced over a disagreement about where to stand their wastebasket. I had remarked to him that they were

165

both sick. Now my wife had left me for a sicker reason I couldn't explain beyond a disagreement over my work hours and political ambition.

The second message had come from Amara Bangali. He had called from Idaho. He figured his call would surprise me. According to his message, he had tried to call a week earlier, but his university had engaged him on several field research trips all that week, which had taken all the strength out of him. In his department, a professor suddenly determined that each of his students must write ten pages on the stories in the news. As a research assistant, he said he had been required to be a support to this professor. However, his breaking news actually was that a university in New York had accepted him into a doctorate program. What did I think about it?

To think of it, Amara Bangali's call was a surprise. The first time I encountered him was when he wanted Yolanda to witness his graduation ceremony. Yolanda had told him he should call me and request that I allow her to attend. After he had called and said he was Amara Bangali who hoped that Yolanda had already mentioned him, I said, "Wrong number," because Yolanda never told me about boys. However, after a clearer explanation followed by a plea, he convinced me to listen to him. Of course, I had agreed at once to let her because I wanted to encourage her to meet someone good for her. As I listened, it became clear to me that she had been merely creating artificial blocks to avoid attending Amara's program. I saw Amara again when he visited my apartment in her company.

Amara and Yolanda had met at a wedding party thrown by a Kaibaran friend of hers who was marrying someone from Belize. It seemed to me that my daughter's attraction to Amara or, for that matter, to any male friend of hers, was not only academic but also ephemeral.

From the first day Amara came to my apartment, I saw his male desire to go to bed with my daughter. He had been introduced as a science graduate. He told me that at twenty-two he had secured an undergraduate degree from the University of Kaibara and had gone on to work as a civil servant. When he explained to me that he'd heard my name mentioned in political circles in Kaibara during his undergraduate days, I was not surprised because I had been a frequent public lecturer in schools and colleges. He said he had to be honest; he came from a financially humble background. His father, a drunkard, had become frustrated over his failure to secure recognition in his chiefdom's administration and had died drowning while trying to catch up with a fishing job in his small river village. His mother was ill and under medical supervision with a doctor in RoMarong City whose fees he paid.

Amara hailed from the southern region of Kaibara. He was of the Mende tribe. He still had bones to pick with certain people in the Kaibara civil service. Because of his bad experience with them, he was doing all he could to return home with as much education as America could provide him. I often wished he were my son.

167

My tow company delivered my car to me in an hour. I had already called my mechanic who promised to pick it up the next day to work on it. I returned my daughter's call, but her cell phone was busy. I left her a voice mail. Amara came on the line as soon as I rang his number. It was as if he had been sitting by his phone, waiting for my call.

"Mr. Johnson! Listen, why don't I call you back? I should pay for this long distance call."

I agreed and hung up. Meanwhile I fidgeted in my pocket and came out with the name of the cab driver, Bundeh Kargbo. His name didn't sound familiar. I knew it was a common Kaibaran name. In Kaibara, the Kargbos, who could be traced to the north, were mostly of the Themne, Loko, or the Limba tribe. I placed his business card beside the telephone and went to refill my glass of wine. In that instant the phone rang. When I picked it the cabby was on the line.

"Hello, this is a pleasant surprise. How did you get my number? Did I give it to you?" I didn't know what else to say.

"Oh, I didn't tell you I already knew your name before I met you? I only had to meet the owner, and you only had to confirm it. Listen, we've been preparing a list, and I saw your number on it. And having met you in person, I had the instinct to call you first," he sounded lively, not as morose as he had been in the cab.

"I'm sorry, who're 'we,' and what list are you talking about?" I asked.

"Oh, I mean the Kaibaran community in Manhattan. There is this long list before me of every Kaibaran in

168

New York. We are planning a trip to the White House in DC to pile up pressure on the American President."

"Ooh! That's a great idea! What's the pressure about, his possible impeachment?"

"No, it is to prevail on America to intervene in the Kaibaran war to end it now."

Then I heard a click on the line. It was another call coming in. Bundeh had begun saying something I hadn't caught because he was laughing like a wild wind.

"Listen, why don't I call you back?" I asked. "There's another call coming in. I'll call you back soon. I'm expecting this call."

He had hung up his phone by the time I finished talking. I brought Amara on the line. He sounded patient. He apologized for making me wait so long. He had gone to the store to buy a phone card. He thanked me for returning his earlier call. He said he had planned to call anyway before he went to bed that evening. He told me again that he had been accepted into a Ph.D. program in New York. I was happy to hear that and congratulated him. He said he would be in New York over the weekend because he had to defend his research proposal at a colloquium before he began the program. I was tempted out of academic itch to ask what his dissertation topic would be, but I didn't want to hear another word about newts. I told him New York was full of fun and that he would like it here. He didn't disappoint me; before he hung up he inquired about Yolanda. I felt sorry for him. Poor thing, couldn't he let go and concentrate on getting his Ph.D.? I guessed right about what he wanted to hear. I bade him goodbye and said I hoped to hear from him again.

When I called Bundeh, he sounded even livelier. There was somber meringue music at the background. He told me he was in a neighborhood bar hanging out with Puerto Rican friends.

"You know, brother Desmond, this is a way of shedding off some of the bad news from home. Remember I told you in the car I was sick of this war?" he sounded as though we had not hung up since he first called. "Well, I still have my two kids trapped in that bloody hell," he told me.

I didn't know whether to cry or to curse. There was a short pause. I knew he was waiting for my response. I continued to hold back. I nearly told him Kaibara was not a hell, but I knew I was wrong. Talking to New York cabby, one must endure the vulgarity of acquaintance.

"So you see? My heart has been a battlefield since the war began. I have lived with it all these years," he said, falling silent for a while before I heard him sucking his teeth. "Look, I must let you go, Buddy. I'll keep you in touch with the program for the White House. If you want to be a part of it, let me know."

The music pounded heavier on his side. Apparently he didn't find me forthcoming on the phone. He would return to the pleasure of his world of Puerto Rican friends.

"Why don't we hang out this weekend?" I found myself saying. I felt foolish afterwards and wished I could withdraw my request.

"That sounds great to me. Plan it and tell me where we can hang. I know New York well and know a lot of exciting places to hang out."

"I'm actually having a young friend of mine over this weekend. He is a Kaibaran too who is moving over here from Idaho. Maybe we three can hang out for the weekend."

"I sure think he needs to be in some lively city. Who wants to live in Idaho? Wherever is that place in America? It will surely be great to hang out with the kid and you. We need to look after each other here. What is the saying? The more the merrier. I used to have a few of our countrymen to hang out with, but they sort of just drifted away, I don't know where. Anything after New York is a dead end. Perhaps they are all in Idaho. It sounds like a place for dead people, like you would say 'I die oh.'"

He suggested a few places, but the more places he named, the wider our choices, so we decided that we should leave everything for the weekend. He hung up without ceremony. .

I wasn't surprised that the number of Kaibarans living in America had grown so high considering that thousands had escaped from the war. Because of the insular nature of my wife, I had had to turn my back on the many Kaibaran functions around me.

Meanwhile, the situation was deteriorating in Kaibara. The *New York Times* for the first time featured the country on its front page. Gruesome pictures of human misery spread across the sheet. The screaming face of a young woman running away from her dusty village as she gripped her mutilated daughter, dripping blood, sent a chill down my spine. Government forces, the paper said, had launched an offensive against the rebels on the east of the country. Nokoh was to be recaptured at all costs. The cost after a six-day battle was devastating. The rebels made what their spokesman called a tactical withdrawal but denied that government forces had completely recaptured Nokoh.

At the same time, the government spokesman was busy thanking ECOMOG through whose help the diamond town of Nokoh had been recaptured with heavy casualties on the side of the rebels. The government forces said no more than three soldiers were reported dead.

That evening CNN's coverage of the war concentrated on Kaibarans fleeing across the country's borders. A UNHCR official reported the figures of refugees in the neighboring countries to be close to a million. Already the agency was appealing to other countries to help with the rising cost of maintaining the refugees.

The BBC carried a story about Kaibarans living in Greece who were outraged because a ship's crew had allegedly sacrificed eighteen Kaibarans on the high seas after discovering them hiding in one of the bottom compartments of the ship. The protesters said the ship had left the port of RoMarong City agreeing to take all eighteen people to safety in Greece. Because the women among them would not accede to having sex with members of the crew, they had been gunned down and thrown into the sea.

Kaibara remained longer in the news the next day. European airports were at odds with airline officials whose flights from Africa had been carrying Kaibarans and other war-torn nationals who, on arrival in Europe, suddenly declared themselves refugees. In France, for instance, authorities had detained a dozen Kaibarans who they said had entered their country illegally. The Kaibarans claimed refugee status, but the French authorities wouldn't listen to their cases, maintaining that those Kaibarans had flown directly from Ivory Coast that was as stable as France was and could have just as easily offered them asylum.

Kaibarans had also met with resistance in North Africa when Arab countries refused to allow them to use their borders as escape routes into Europe. Most of them, therefore, had been imprisoned. Many of the prisoners complained of being treated worse than animals. They talked about being called derogatory names associating their race with the devil. They told of how they were being forced into slavery, some claiming that they had been blindfolded and marched into remote villages from which they couldn't find their way out.

An Italian reporter also met and spoke with Kaibaran teenagers engaged in prostitution in Trieste. The girls complained of how sailors aboard Italian vessels sailing from RoMarong City had encouraged them go aboard and embark for better lives in Europe. They spoke of how once in Italy these so called good Samaritans had starved them unless they agreed to offer themselves as prostitutes in clandestine nightclubs. Way down in South Africa, a company had completed a contract to send white South African mercenaries to help the government prosecute the war. Mercenaries with the company, Executive Outcomes, had arrived in Kaibara with their eyes wide open and as bright as the diamonds they hoped to exploit.

Along a provincial highway two international reporters were found dead. The homelands of these two reporters, Canada and the United States, reported to the world via documentaries that Kaibara had suddenly become the worst place in the world for anyone to live. Rebels blamed the reporters' deaths on government soldiers. The spokesman said, "The government sacrificed these innocent men to keep their secrets secret."

In another development, the government accused the international Red Cross of supporting the rebels. The organization had tried to defend itself with rhetoric of its policy of neutrality. The government wasn't impressed, so it released a statement identifying "five dubious Red Cross officials" who were ordered to vacate the country within twenty-four hours.

Five days later, the government of the United Kingdom advised its citizens that Kaibara was no longer a safe place to live. The World Bank announced from the United States that it was suspending a loan that had been approved three months earlier for the country at its August meeting. The Breton Woods institution concluded that the loan was likely to fall in the wrong hands. Kaibara had become ungovernable!

I first learned about the most recent coup from Amara. He had called in the middle of the night to break the news to me. He mentioned something about the birth of a revolution. Thirty minutes later, Bundeh was on the line weeping for his children in Kaibara. He spoke into the phone as though I had the power to reverse the coup and order that his family be removed from the country at once. He kept reminding me it was a military coup in case I had suddenly lost the meanings of the words in my head. Noticing I was helpless, he began convincing himself that the international community would rebuke the plotters and that they would not have the necessary support to hold on long to power. I agreed with him. He must have sucked his teeth four or five times. I politely suggested that we both monitor the news properly to keep track of things as they unfolded. Reluctantly, he agreed to it, sucked his teeth again, bade me farewell, and hung up the phone. It was a relief. I switched on my television to CNN and poured myself a red wine. I loved my wine chilly so I put in some ice cubes and returned to settle close to the television.

Five Palestinians had just been reported killed as they tried to defend their motherland with slings and stones and bombs strapped to their bodies against the sophistication of the Israelis. An angry PLO spokesman was calling for the world to condemn the Israeli occupation of their land. The anchorman returned to what he called breaking news.

The screen showed a still life photograph of the presidential mansion in RoMarong City. A military coup had just been reported in the small West African country of Kaibara. The president had been ousted in the early hours of the morning, and his whereabouts were yet unknown. It could be recalled that the president was on record for admitting that he had been a failure. Gunshots could be heard in the capital city of RoMarong City. No one had yet taken responsibility for the coup, but soldiers in military fatigues could be seen moving up and down the streets. The anchorman said he was afraid that that was all he had then but promised to bring more information as it came in.

NYC woke four hours later to a bright day; its fringes were unaware of what had taken place in the small West African country of Kaibara far across the Atlantic where the sun scorched the land year round. My next class was supposed to be on that day, but I quickly called my learners to explain to them I wouldn't be available. The Spanish couple said it was a shame this could happen in the country of their fine teacher. They hoped my relatives there were safe. The Ukrainian breathed heavily on the line and said, "*Tak, tak, tak.*" He added that, honestly, he was not surprised about the coup. I felt that he was right, given the recent bad news. He said it was not for that reason; he just thought Kaibara was in a deep shit. He said the trouble with Kaibara was that the international community just chose to ignore it. He concluded that Kaibara was a wonderful country the world knew nothing about. How would he know that? I was surprised and deeply moved by his assessment. I guess he was only being compassionate.

"I thought soldiers were too busy to have time to follow up on things outside their terrain," I said, unable to contain my surprise.

"I know, I know, Mr. Johnson," he said with an effortless laughter. "But me, I am sorry for you. Take sorry, Mr. Johnson, take sorry."

I had no time to give him the usual reminder to cut the Mr. Johnson crap and call me Desmond. Instead, I just thanked him and hung up.

Bundeh called ten minutes later. He wasn't going to drive his cab that day for anyone, so he was spending the entire day at home monitoring the news as I advised him. He had also learned from the organizing group of the Kaibara community in New York that the intended march to the White House to pressure the American government into intervening in the internal affairs of Kaibara had been postponed. He also had a bit of information to pass on. His wife's brother had called from RoMarong City describing the situation there as grave. He had confirmed that a coup had taken place and that he wanted money for him and the kids to go to a neighboring country. I shut my eyes to imagine how tense my newfound friend must be. Then he added, "My children are safe though, but I think their mother is away from them. Well, that is as usual."

"Thank God for your children, but why is your wife's disappearance usual?"

"No, no, no, Mabinty's behavior—that's the mother of my children in RoMarong City, and she is my former wife. She is never with the children. God knows where

177

she'd be in that hell. I fear that her immoral behavior would endanger the kids, which is why I'm worried."

As soon as I hung up the phone, the coup was announced on my television.

13

*The narrator came to me in my dream whispering
in my ear that the long story was coming to an end.
He said it would not be long the body of reality was
going to merge with the body of Kabara's entire
narrative. He said to me that all of what he had
told me was going to soon appear to me as a
winding road, a road that I had been traveling
through the last thirty years. He ended the long
story by telling me about the road. He called it the
road to Kaibara:*

Borbor Pain had fallen out with all the founding
members of the movement. After the death of Manure
and Raster, all others, whether they were from the
council or from Libya, no longer dared visit him in the
bush any more. He learned the nuances of the

179

movement keenly during all the trips he had made around the world in the company of Manure and Raster. While many of those he met supported the military course, they had felt strongly against using it, so after the death of Manure and Raster they seemed to fall by the way side. He had to open his own international network afresh.

His confidant from RoMarong City, the unassuming Lebanese businessman, Abess Bittar walked in with two white men. He hugged Borbor Pain and praised him for his success in taking over Nokoh. He introduced the two men in his company. They smiled broadly and reached for Borbor Pain's hand. The two men were successful Eastern European businessmen with offices in Antwerp.

"This is the great revolutionary I told you about. You can see it around him, the greatness of Mahatma Gandhi and the vigor of Martin Luther King, Jr.," Abess said. His accomplices again reached for the hand of Borbor Pain more vehemently than before.

"Well," Borbor Pain said, "we are a people's revolution. We have followed the suffering of our people and are responding to their wish."

The two European businessmen were visiting to conduct business. It was not their concern to interfere with what Borbor Pain was doing for or against his people. They were perfect war businessmen. They told him about the many deals they'd had in the Congo, Uganda, Somalia, and various countries in Asia.

180

"So this place is now under your control?" one of them asked, looking about the room as though it was all there was to Nokoh.

"The entire district is in under my control and I'm now heading for RoMarong City. But after the recent skirmishes we need to recoup before we continue our journey."

Borbor Pain took out a carefully wrapped white handkerchief from inside a side box and opened it. Satisfied, he spread it on the table and called his guests around him. The three men walked over and beheld the cleanest and most attractive diamonds they had seen in all their business careers. For a while they were silent, casting their eyes only on the magnificence of the diamonds.

"Touch them, feel them. My father used to call them 'Karafilo's stones.' One Kaibaran writer called them 'The mocking stones.' Aren't they great?" Borbor Pain imagined Manure over them with his condescending call of "Corporal."

Now he made every decision singularly. He had been thinking about his plans to march into RoMarong City. He knew that the diamonds would help him with his dream.

"They may be tiny stones, yet they are wonderful?" the East European said.

"They are bigger than any ones I have seen in the world market," Borbor Pain lied.

The East European changed his demeanor when he realized how much the rebel leader knew about international diamond sales. The diamonds were indeed

181

valuable and could garner large bids in Antwerp.
Borbor Pain was a man with whom he wanted to do
business

"Abess must have let you all known how I'm
determined to part with these stones. Our organization
doesn't want to do business with every Jack and Jill.
We want to have a partner. We want cash as well as
ammunition. You must be aware of how much the
government is sabotaging our arms transfer from other
countries. I am prepared to be reasonable with you if
you will support my international arms network."

There was a total silence. No one spoke. All eyes
rested on the sparkling diamonds. The East Europeans
had never indulged in arms trafficking. Nor had they
ever beheld diamonds as magnificent as those before
them. With their knowledge in illicit diamonds, arms
trafficking for one organization might not pose a
problem, what with all the beautiful Kaibaran diamonds
they had heard about. They looked up in excitement.

"Who do you already have on your team?" the East
European asked.

"You are going to form that team. Abess and I on this
side, and you abroad will be part of the team," Borbor
Pain gently rubbed the diamonds between his palms.

"Then we have to call for a partnership of equal
percentage," the East European ventured.

"Now you are talking!" exclaimed Borbor Pain.
"That's the kind of business I had in mind. My primary
aim is to reach RoMarong City and seize power as soon
as possible. So I have no problem with that."

The East Europeans thought they made a good deal. They placed a briefcase on the table and opened it to expose thousands of dollars in neat packets. Then they put another briefcase on the table.

"We have been very smart to come along with communications equipment. This represents the latest in technology on the market. We will need to have it for code communication. Abess will come again in the next two weeks, if it's fine with you, to help install it."

"We shall draw up an agreement, a Memorandum of Understanding, between your organization and ours," said Borbor Pain. "I think Abess must travel to Antwerp in the next two weeks for that," he paused, and then added, "Abess will be traveling with my spokesman who is already in England. And I am hoping to have a spokesman of Kaibaran origin who is based in the United States"

That evening, Borbor Pain had enough money to dish out to his henchmen. His men were busy having a good time in the camp, not knowing that while they celebrated, their leader was negotiating with the strangers. There was enough to eat and drink. When the businessmen were gone, Borbor Pain went out of his office to address his fighters. He told them about the guests he had received.

"People in other parts of the world who have seen our struggle in their television screens have vowed to help us."

The crowd went wild.

"These are people who have been following the political history of Kaibara. They are aware of the injustices and human rights violation of the government. They know about the many injustices going on in this country. Wishing to help, they sent a team of three white men this afternoon from Europe to have a word with me—to assure me of their support for our struggle."

The crowd cheered again.

"They didn't believe they would find so many of you here. They thought our revolution was only a small group of people as the government had led them to believe. They were impressed with your number, your effort, your resolve, and, above all, your commitment."

The crowd went wild again.

Borbor Pain paused and waited for the noise to die down. "For every revolutionary in this movement, the guests have left behind money."

As the crowd burst out in excited shouts, two men dashed forward and lifted Borbor Pain onto their shoulders and began to dance about with him.

Merriment characterized the evening, as the November moon shone on them with eyes of silver dust.

Borbor Pain had just solved his major worries. For the first time, he could now dismiss Macknoon and Brian and their foreign partners who had not showed up since the death of Manure and Raster. They knew his wireless line, but they hadn't contacted him. In his mind, he simply said good riddance. He was in fact never comfortable in conducting ammunition deals with women who wore wild jeans and moved unsteadily about like maniacal pigs posing to be vegans.

At that moment, Superman briskly walked over to him with a radio firmly clutched in his hand. After Grabo's escape, which to the surprise of his men Borbor Pain had never commented on, he had made Superman, his number two man.

"Did you hear that?" Superman asked, almost falling on him.

"What? I don't have my radio with me?" Borbor Pain said.

"Here you are!" Superman gave Borbor Pain his portable.

Superman turned to the rowdy rebels and shouted one loud slogan to which a unanimous response rang from all corners of the open field followed by a deep silence. His voice indeed carried weight. If a mosquito were buzzing about, it would have been heard in the grave.

Loud and clear, the BBC reported that the vulnerable Kaibaran government in RoMarong City had fallen to the hands of a young and unknown renegade captain fighting the rebel forces of the Corporal in what was described as "a bloodless military coup."

Borbor Pain smashed the radio in disbelief. Placing his two hands on top of his head, he felt the pains of being a political loser all his years as he felt hot solidified tears going down his bruised cheeks.

"Another bastard ahead of me!" he bellowed, swallowing thick foam of spittle. "My countrymen don't learn any lesson. When I'm finished with them, there shall be no place called RoMarong City!"

He didn't quite believe himself. He knew how much pain his life had been through for this one hunger of ruling his country by any means necessary. How he was almost there, succeeding with the first, even with the second attempt...but for the errors of his squad mates and their neglect of paying attention to the details. He wished he had gunned the officer who cried like a baby after hitting his head against a wall in the darkness...rousing up a security who otherwise would have been murdered in his sleep. He had particularly urged the others to leave out that awkward officer of the plan, but he had been outnumbered in the quick vote that followed. And he had come and spoilt his chances of succeeding in his second coup attempt. But perhaps his most excruciating pain of all was the thought of managing a war against the military of his country; a military that had made him and had destroyed him. His adventures, in the past, in the present and in the future, he thought, seemed to be characterized by an unending pain.

The narrator waved me goodbye. He stood at the door and disappeared into thin air.

14

I had gone into exile in a rather bizarre circumstance. I left RoMarong City in the middle of the night inside a small boat. The French vessel that was to help me reach the neighboring country didn't show up in time for my escape. Even after I had gone, I kept asking by phone to my cousin who had stood by me that evening if the vessel showed up later.

Looking back on my fears then, I figured I had pushed the stakes too high. I also knew that anything could happen considering that only a few years into his rule, my president had fallen out with all of his henchmen, particularly after the coup. The reward for my apprehension was so high that I had feared even my relatives would have been tempted to betray their own blood and make money out of me. Not even my wife knew the depth of my plans. While I kept her at bay, I

187

continued to arrange for how she was to join me in the neighboring country once I arrived there.

The fear of being sabotaged had sent me to negotiate with one of the local fishermen to help me secure any secret passage he knew about to the neighboring country. He had first stared at me and wanted to know why I so urgently wanted to go away to the neighboring country in the middle of the night in an unpardonable rain. Obviously, it was clear that the man didn't know me and didn't know about the fiery demand on my head printed in all the papers. Without mentioning the ransom, I told him that some people in the government were after my life because I had good thoughts against their bad thoughts for the country.

Five days earlier, my wife and I had escaped from the comfort of our home, groping our way through a bitter rain. It had poured as though it meant to sound an alarm announcing our escape from the gang that had broken into the front door while guarding the back to prevent our flight.

My wife and I had squeezed through a rustic kitchen window whose frame had been blackened by the smoke of her daily broil. I had jumped out first and then had helped her out. We had no idea where we were going to, but we had to leave the scene quickly before the flame that had been ignited in our sitting room exposed our already fume-darkened images in the rain.

We must have walked the streets for thirty minutes before we realized that we had nowhere safe to go. My trusted friend, Archibald Cole, had just been arrested for a repeated time. We had to keep going. I decided it

188

was not safe for the two of us to be together. She had a cousin living somewhere in the ruined ghettoes of the seaside. Normally I would not have left her to risk it alone, but the fear of being caught together distressed us. I felt she had a better chance without me.

I gave her a quick kiss and the promise of my love. I urgently instructed her to send someone to the American Ambassador with a note in which she should indicate her whereabouts. I cautioned her that the note might fall in the wrong hands. I accompanied her down to the bay as we felt our way through the slums.

Yolanda Granville-Sharp, my wife's cousin, had an impressive European compound surname admired in Kaibara, but she didn't conduct herself in a manner worthy of it. She had left school at an early age to hang out with foreigners who came and left in boats from communist countries. Very soon, she and others carried the nick name, *Sanka Maru,* taken from a Japanese boat crisscrossing Asia and Africa in the early 60s with cheap and inferior items. However, she later made a name for herself as a community activist for our political party after I introduced her to the president. She had gathered the bay women, organized them into a strong force, and fished considerable votes from them to help us win the elections. However, after the elections that brought in the president of Kaibara, she tried in vain countless times to gain favors from the government. I myself tried at one time to put in a word for her, reminding the president about his promise to her, but he had frustrated my effort when he told me he didn't remember her and was in fact too busy to discuss her anytime.

She became a recluse who found solace only in alcohol.

Reaching her door at the bay, I told my wife I ought to be moving on, but she scolded me, asking whether I would really leave her to be killed in the rain in that godforsaken darkness. I asked her to wait as I tapped on Yolanda Granville-Sharp's door and whispered her name. As the bolt rudely groaned and labored to unlock in the quiet night, I breathed a sigh of relief and almost set off to find my own hiding, but my wife told me I had to kiss her again.

In that instant, the door opened widely and suddenly stopped. My wife said goodbye as she stepped inside. There was a loud scream even before I took a first step to disappear into the dark. Inside the small and silent room lay Yolanda Granville-Sharpe, dead. I elbowed my way in and looked quickly around. No one else was in the room. Who then had opened the door for us? Who had killed Yolanda Granville-Sharpe in that thick night? Many years later, convinced that the president had butchered her in pursuit of my life, we agreed to name our daughter after her.

The reign of terror under Kaibara's first president began screening in layers of clouds. Six months into his reign, two opposition party members were perishing at the Dembapa Prison. They had been arrested while attending parliamentary meetings. They were not charged with anything, but they had been targeted with

190

the vague allegation that they had been disturbing the national peace the president was fighting so hard to maintain. How had they done this? They questioned the president's proposal to change vehicular traffic from left hand to right hand. The two MPs had considered the change a rebellious departure from the good efforts of the colonial masters.

In prison, they declared a hunger strike until they were tried. Four days into their strike action, one of them died. Because he had not been considered a criminal, his cold body was handed over to his family.

The opposition party brought up the issue in parliament and expressed their concern that they and their family members no longer felt safe. Parliament dismissed their fears. As for the MP who had died in incarceration, the ruling party's MPs had argued that the government pathologist's report stated that the MP's death was the result of a long illness that had been threatening his life. The report described the dead colleague as terminally ill and stated that he was going to die in any circumstances.

As for the other one still in prison, whose release was being advocated, parliament reminded opposition colleagues not to forget the president's due respect for the separation of powers. The judiciary, they said, still considered the MP a threat to social order and that it would be unconstitutional for government to try to obstruct the business of or to dictate to the competent judiciary what to do. However, the Speaker of the House promised the opposition that the parliament, which he took pains to describe as the voice of the people, would pressure the judiciary and appeal to the president for a quick trial of their colleague.

However, not only did the opposition colleague continue to stay in incarceration, but also more joined him. That was how Archibald Cole, my friend, found himself repeatedly in jail where he died many years later. Soon the newspapers turned the issue into a daily story. These papers too dug holes for themselves. The troubles had begun as firestorms that consumed the buildings of two newspaper offices. A month later, journalists were going in and out of prisons as though they were at a funfair.

Persecutions were a new development in independent Kaibara. We had just entered the second decade of political freedom. Many people who didn't suspect the government's intention to silence its critics confused the abuses for a positive presidential activism to motivate Kaibarans whom they said had become too used to British colonial lackadaisical providence. The radio lauded the president for his "union spiritualism and spiritual unionism" and reminded its listeners that the new president was bringing into politics the life he had brought into the railway union while he was leader there.

Regardless of the exploitation, the British had left behind a body of governmental example robust enough to catapult the nation to success. When our government assumed political power, it inherited a sound social and economic foundation. We formed a government in an atmosphere of political pluralism. In those days, while the Asian economy was struggling to survive, ours competed with those of the British and the United States. Our currency was strong with the backing of the British pound. No one wanted the American dollar, which was many cents below the nation's currency.

During this time, Kaibara became home to many refugees from Southern Africa. Racism and apartheid were sowing gelatinous roots in the black communities of those countries. The commonwealth and other international organizations provided support to African countries that opted to accept black students who were not matriculated into white owned universities in their home countries. Together, with countries like Nigeria and Ghana, Kaibara became an elder state over South Africa, Rhodesia, and Lesotho, helping to educate its future black leaders and intellectuals.

The president gave me a special, international assignment to monitor events in the Southern African countries. I was to work with their foreign students and refugees and advise the president on sharp policies against their racist rule. For the most part, I had nothing to do. There was certainly and directly nothing Kaibara could do to change situations in those countries all by itself. As a result of my assignment, even though it was below that of a cabinet rank, I had the opportunity of close-quarter contact with members of the diplomatic community. Among my closest colleagues was the American Ambassador. His country wanted any support it could get for its Southern African policies and the cold war it was engaged in with the

Russians. My imminent idleness and lack of job challenge gave me time to pry into other issues affecting my country. However, through these extra-curricular activities a bad blood was created between the president and me.

It all began after I attended a symposium entitled "Democracy in Diversity," organized by the United States Information Agency. The Ambassador had served as the chairman. I had been asked to present the lead paper in which I projected the future of pluralism in the two states of Kaibara and South Africa. At the end of my presentation, the Ambassador didn't contain his good impression of me.

"That paper is *so* prophetic," he had said over tea. "I strongly believe in it. My Director of the USIA is faxing a copy of it to State Department. And if you like, I think we can fund a broader dissemination of your paper through your country's mass media."

"I would love that, Mr. Ambassador, but you know the President insists on knowing matters like these before we give consent."

"Oh. I know that, Desmond. I'm looking forward to hearing from you on that soon. Just don't forget that the embassy can do this program on its own without having to consult with your government. You know it is part of the foreign policy of the US Government, but I want you in, so I'm sure going to let you discuss it with your government."

I noticed the Ambassador said "government" where I said "president." I found his proposal exciting: it would be a way, at least, for me to keep busy. By the nature of my job, I was classified as a non-essential staff member in the government, a status that worried me after all I had done to see our party into power. Before naming his cabinet, the president had tapped me as the possible Minister of Justice, but when the time came to make a choice, he had announced a junior lawyer for the office. I felt it was a betrayal, and I had been uneasy ever since.

"I'm positive it's going to work, Mr. Ambassador," I said. "I just want my president to know I'll be gone for a couple of days in case he wants me to do some other thing. With our leaders, you never know when an emergency is on the way," I tried to create an image of myself as important and busy.

The Ambassador, however, was not one to mince words. "We can plan the week long program to engage you. There's not much you do that I know of," he giggled and tapped me on the back while winking at me.

His words irritated me. I noticed his bespectacled eyes seeing through my soft skin. I nearly dropped my glass and walked out of the embassy auditorium. I felt his grip on my arm as he pulled me to a confidential corner.

"Desmond, I have recommended you for a six weeks fellowship in Washington. I believe that you are essential in the new dispensation. It will be an insult to your legal professional standing if you don't help correct it now."

New dispensation?

As for the fellowship, I wholeheartedly accepted, only I still wanted to impress on him how important I was to the president who would find it difficult to release me. Because I agreed with him that there has to be a new

195

dispensation, I took a deep breath, sipped my coffee, and preferred to be honestly genuine with him.

When he noticed I had nothing to say, he again patted me on the back and interpreted my silence as consent.

He then dipped into his breast pocket. "There's only one man in your government who has a direct access to my residential phone: your president. Take it. I think we have a lot to discuss."

Before he left me for the company of some journalists who were waiting to chat with him, he said, "Let me know tomorrow when you think the program should commence."

It can start now, Mr. Ambassador," I felt like saying. *It's time to fight back!*

15

My secretary told me that the call came directly from the president.

The president!

My mind instantly raced to the American Ambassador. The president had not called me directly in a long while, and I hadn't seen him for months. My instructions had been to discuss all official matters with him through his spokesman, a very fussy official whom no one below cabinet level bypassed. Now, a direct call from the president. Why would he bypass his spokesman to call me? The American Ambassador. Had he misquoted me to the president? Was he a spy for my president? Why would an American ambassador party with my president? My mind began to race to the possible deals of diamonds, gold, bauxite, contracts, what?

I picked up the phone as I recalled a party member who had only recently died mysteriously at his residence the day he fell out with the president. Everyone knew the president hated him, and that he had called the shot.

"Desmond, are you there?"

"Yes, Mr. President!"

"If you can make it, come to my office now. I want us to discuss this over wine."

I told him I would be right there and thanked him graciously. I listened until he had dropped his receiver.

I sighed and burst out with a roar of laughter. I knew the tone of my president when it was generous. There it was at last. Before he became president, he had always admired the culture of number ten Downing Street nominations of the British Prime Minister's cabinet. He had told us then during the campaigns that if after the elections he requested someone's presence over the phone, then that someone was marked for an office. It was only that with the president, the call would not say which office on the phone. He just said—what was it? He said, "If you can make it, come to my office now." It had been said he could name a man to five cabinet offices before the man showed up.

I called my wife. She answered the phone in the kitchen.

"I will be late today, honey!" I said in one breath.

"Why? What would you be doing?"

"The president just called me on his direct line. He thinks we should have a discussion over wine," I tried not to sound excited.

"Is that right?" What are you waiting for?" I could sense her excitement. "My God, I can't believe this is happening to us. What do you think, honey?"

"I really don't know now. I'm just confused. We better leave it at that until I come home."

"Maybe it's a shake-up, and you know…"

"Honey, let's just leaves it at that for now. There are many lines in a telephone. Let's only be hopeful."

"You deserve the best, honey. You deserve it."

We sent kisses, and I hung up.

I dialed a friend's number, but when his voice came on, I dropped the handset. I thought if anything, it should be a surprise to him. I began to dial the Ambassador's number. I gave it up and returned the paper with his number on it to my wallet. Could he have been the catalyst? I dialed M'balu's number. It was her sister who picked up the phone and told me she was not in.

I kept a mirror in the office to polish up before going anywhere. It was M'balu's idea that I had it in the office. She had also bought me a comb, a spray, and a deodorant. She always said she wanted her lover to look just right anywhere I went, except when I stood before my wife.

What elevation does the president have for me? Would he have read in my disposition that I was not at all happy with the Southern African thing he made for me? I was so disappointed when he came up with the idea. For two days he was not sure of how to designate the position. He had come up with several names.

199

"No, we cannot call it 'Ambassador.' It is not really anything like that. My idea is to toe the line of the United Nations, and have the world powers mention us in their good books. Why don't we call it 'Special Representative to Southern Africa?' But wait a minute. You are not really going to be based in that region. Look, why don't you and I think it over and talk about it in three weeks."

In three weeks!

I thought the president was insensitive to my feelings. However, my wife and I spent a night making up names. We borrowed books from the library and tried to think about counterparts in other countries.

"Let's begin by describing what you would be doing in the office," my wife had said.

"Honey, I have no idea. I guess I will be following the political events in those countries and reporting to the president."

"That would make you a government reporter," my wife joked.

"Yeah, maybe a spy," I said.

"But what is the purpose? What is the motivation of your investigation?" my wife had asked.

I hated the word investigation. It sounded to me like I was being made an armchair police of some place thousands of miles away. I had not disclosed to my wife that the president had created the position only to please western powers and not to compensate me for my hard work and for my worth in the party. I had felt funny and empty.

That evening, the national radio began reading the list of the new cabinet of the new president. Each time a name was called, my heart skipped a beat. I felt like I had been used, abused, and dumped. Many of the cabinet names were not active party members. Two of the ministers were people who defected from the opposition. And there I was, a staunch member, left in the cold.

What was wrong with the president? Why did he leave me out of his cabinet? Many of my Krio folks had cautioned me earlier to take it easy with what they called the provincial parties or parties of the natives. I began to think I had been bypassed as a result of my ethnic minority affiliation, but I hated to think that way. After all, there were Krios in the cabinet. I felt uneasy with even my wife who chose to believe in the ethnic reasoning. She had fumed all night and hated everything the party stood for. She even hated herself. I felt so embarrassed that night thinking about how my private staff was expecting they were going to move with me to a bigger and more prestigious office.

After the cabinet announcement, the telephone must have rung forever, but neither my wife nor I picked it. We put out the lights in the sitting room and lost our appetites for dinner, which lay wasted on the dining table all night.

I counted myself not as a founding member but as a senior member of the party. I registered when it was in its creeping stage. On returning from Britain, I had met with offers to team with other young lawyers to institute a law firm.

But I discovered a political atmosphere that was very inviting. The ruling party was enjoying success. The British had continued to hang around Kaibara, still nurturing it. The two countries had not parted as enemies as it would later happen with countries of Southern Africa. We had received our independence on a silver platter at Queen Elizabeth's finest hour. She even went so far as to knight some of our founding fathers.

In the wake of our independence, many trade unions had emerged and lent their voices to the political issues of the day. A vanguard of brilliant newspapers also emerged, their editors writing fine commentaries. There was no need for hostility. There were no instances of brutality.

Soon, because of our agricultural success, Kaibara began exporting rice to neighboring countries. By that time, a strong West African alliance had seen our educated folks employed or contracted in neighboring countries to serve as judges, state medical doctors, and environmentalists. In Nigeria, for instance, there was a good number of Kaibarans holding senior federal government positions.

RoMarong City largely copied the European model of conducting its social affairs. The Queen of England respected the city mayor. Rumor had it that she visited London every month in order to learn how to improve the social outlook of her city.

RoMarong City busied itself Monday through Friday, and on Saturday, it organized a number of activities to entertain its citizens. The British Council was one spot where mostly European plays were staged. Occasionally, plays written by Kaibarans were put on stage also. There was the City Park named after the royal Victoria. People were encouraged to hang out there as long as they upheld the unedited European bylaws pasted at the entrance gates.

On Sunday the city rested.

It was to this RoMarong City that I returned after my studies in England. I had arrived after the death of the first Prime Minister. Power had just been handed to his brother who was not as favored as his late brother was. For one thing, everyone considered the selection of the late man's brother a blatant show of nepotism and tribalism sanctioned by the party.

These undemocratic practices caused bad blood in the nation. The brother himself didn't help the situation with his lackadaisical attitude of addressing state issues. He didn't have confidence in the loyalty of his citizens whom he thought didn't care about him being Prime Minister.

It was then that my party was born!

The president had made a name for himself in the railway union. He had controlled it as though it was his personal property. He organized it with such creativity that it became a very powerful pressure group. By this time, the common loyalty to the idea of a nation state was waning, and the ruling party had lost the ability to hold the nation together. The country was falling apart.

One day the president, before he became president, went to listen to a speech I gave at the invitation of the bar association and after that he invited me to his union office to discuss "issues of national importance," as he put it.

I had gone to see him on the approved day.

"I don't often tell people they make fine speeches, because I have a competitive spirit, and I make fine speeches myself."

That was how he greeted me at the entrance of his office.

"I will take it as a complement," I said to him as we entered his office.

His office was dark and without a cooling system.

"I understand you are a good lawyer," he said.

Could that be the reason why this big-headed man has called me to his office? I told him I was a lawyer who had studied in England.

"I too studied in England: a British institution on a British scholarship."

Fine, Mister, I felt like saying. Instead I asked, "Is that why I am here?"

"Look, I don't like to delay matters, because I am a busy man. The new party has asked me to talk to you about offering you a membership." He paused. "They want you on board to act as the party lawyer."

I later learned it was a big lie. I felt he didn't want me to know how highly he had regarded me.

"You are aware of the blunders of this new Prime Minister. He doesn't have the same respect for the rule of law as his elder brother, the late man, may his soul rest in peace."

Two weeks later I accepted the invitation and left my law partnership, for the other partners didn't want to meddle with politics.

16

My clock struck three. I gathered up the day's work ten minutes after the president had called. He was going to see me in the absence of his spokesperson.

I told my driver to knockoff early that day. I told him I would drive myself home. I was soon in my car heading for the presidential State House. The market stalls teamed with buyers and sellers. The shouts of child hawkers could be heard all over the place. There stood piles of rubbish in every corner discharging a bad odor in the air and close to each pile of rubbish was a madman or a beggar occasionally picking from the piles. The city had changed indeed.

I negotiated a small slope that led to the presidential State House where the streets were neatly paved and carpet grass grew on each side of them. Servants could be seen watering the grass and picking up trash that they wouldn't pick from their own bodies.

Five guards were assigned to the main gates that opened for vehicular traffic. Three others stood on each side of the drive to examine papers. I drove and stopped before three other men who conducted a search of my vehicle. Then I drove into the compound where two ladies sat in a cell-like cubicle and demanded to know my mission to the House. I was asked to leave an identification card with them and wear a visitor's tag around my neck. I then waited for two people who eventually ushered me into a big waiting room after conducting a disgusting search on my body.

Didn't these people recognize me? I asked myself. Although I had not been to the State House for a long time, yet I thought I was so useful in the party that presidential guards should have been able to identify me on sight. After all, I visited there regularly before that cow of a spokesman was appointed from God knows where.

I was able to see the president after three hours. He had just met with a group of Muslim clerics who were campaigning for the recognition of Islam as a state religion. Rumor had it that some Arab countries rich in oil were pushing the issue. No one ever actually knew what the president believed in, just as no one really knew his ethnicity.

"For how long have you been waiting, Desmond? Why, you should have just walked right into my office," the president said, appearing behind me.

I looked into his eyes to determine if he really didn't mean to kill me in his office after all because I had no idea how I was supposed to walk into his office with all the guns of his militia brandished all over the place.

Yes, he had a militia guarding him. By this time, he had weakened the military and carved from it a body of armed men that he first called the ISU, or Internal Security Unit. After a year, he organized a national banquet to change the name to SSD, the Special Security Division. He divided the rest of the army, handpicked from it a few authorities, and sat them in the corridors of political power from where he would later discover the man he eventually made succeeded him as president. He removed the ammunition from all soldiers and distanced himself from them. While still a young lieutenant, the next president was made head of the unit.

It was this unit he said I should have disregarded and walk right into his office, majestically.

I simply smiled and turned to face him.

"Sit down, Desmond. I have not had time to ask you how the monitoring assignment is going with—what do you call it?"

"Southern Africa!" I quickly put in. I began to wonder again if in fact he knew anything about my job.

"Ah, yes, Southern Africa. I will like to visit those countries to have a firsthand experience of how black people are treated there. But you know, being a busy president is not a pleasant thing to think about."

Why don't you just pack your bag and leave? I thought.

"You, a younger man, have very little to worry about, but at my age, I ought to be resting a lot. Yet how can I?"

You are not indispensable, mister, I thought. What do you think will happen when you die? I said to myself.

"You see, I keep telling every Kaibaran how lucky they are in this part of the world. What with the discrimination blacks suffer in England and America? What with the apartheid in South Africa? Yet with all this peace I have given this country like showers of blessings, people continue to delve into deserts of evil only to hurt me."

I was so angry with the big-headed, good-for-nothing president. If I'd had a gun then, I believe I would have shot him dead. He gave me a fierce look as though he read my thought.

He asked me what I felt.

I found myself gushing like a stupid man. "I think, sir, that you are right. We don't have any excuse to try to divide our country. You should be considered a peacemaker."

He sprang from his chair in excitement. "That's it, Desmond! That's the right outlook! Dividing this country won't help anyone."

Was I shocked? No, I was baffled with the entire conversation. I had visited the president, ready to learn about my nomination to a cabinet position, and here I was listening to analogy to America and South Africa. Nevertheless, I continued to be patient as I was certain to take home an appointment letter.

"Desmond, I called you here to talk about state matters."

My heart pounded. I felt my blood rushing through my veins. I tried to swallow, but my throat was dry. I looked him directly in the eye. I thought about the wine he had mentioned on the phone. He had not offered it to me yet, but who needed wine when a miracle was on the way?

"I am at your service, Mr. President!" To my own ears I sounded like a starving dog looking at a covered dish my owner had just removed from the refrigerator.

"I see the opposition is engaged in a conspiracy to sabotage my government."

There it was. The master touched the cover, and I was now wagging my tail. What was it going to be? Was it the ministry of Internal Affairs to put some sense into the opposition? Or was it the ministry of Constitutional Affairs, not a very lucrative department, but to put some security in the constitution?

"It is too bad for our young democracy, Mr. President?" I breathed. The dog in me was licking its chops.

"We must gather our team to fight against it."

The aroma was arousing. I salivated. Tell me the good news now, Mr. President! I wanted to shout. "Don't treat me this way, I cannot hold out much longer!"

"Mr. Johnson," the president said sternly.

Why had he changed from calling me "Desmond?" Was the status coming now? *H.E. Mr. Johnson Johnson, Esq. Minister of . . .*

210

I had written that phrase in five blank papers three hundred times after the telephone call. I left them sprawling on top of my office table.

"Mr. Johnson," he repeated.

The telephone on his table rang. He picked it up and after a while breathed into it and said, "Fine!"

"Mr. Johnson, I have been waiting for the others to come; now, we have everyone here. We really need to have a way of changing the system in this country in favor of a one party democracy. That's why I have called you here."

I nearly fainted. The master overturned an empty dish. The dog in me squealed.

"Well, gentlemen, I'd like to welcome you all to my office. I must confess Mr. Johnson and I have already started the discussion. I think it would be good if you just join us," the president said, rising to welcome his Ministers of Constitutional Affairs, of Justice, and of Internal Affairs.

As they took their seats, I rose to shake hands with each one of them.

"The point is, gentlemen, if I must continue, we have the right to protect the constitution, but to preserve a constitution that is not dynamic is tantamount to sleeping at night with all of one's doors open to thieves," The president went directly to the point.

"In other words, Mr. President, you are right to say it is like inviting thieves to locate and cart away what they want," the Minister of Constitutional Affairs said, as if he had been with us from the start. He made himself so unofficially free with the president.

"Is it not written in the good book that one does not put one's new wine in an old wine skin?" the Justice Minister added.

"As a matter of fact, that is a nice quote. I'll use it to introduce our new concept in my countrywide tour," said the president. "Only I'll put it the other way round: you cannot put an old wine in a new wineskin."

"I agree that it makes more sense that way," the Justice Minister quickly accepted with a sheepish smile.

"Mr. President, we wouldn't be talking here if we didn't think that we as the new wineskin are already bursting our seams," said the Internal Affairs Minister with his wry smile.

"Talking about it, in fact, reminds me of the wine I have reserved for this meeting," the president pushed a button on his intercom and a minute later a lady was approaching our table with a tray of the finest wine money could buy.

I felt uncomfortable to think that what I was learning only then that the issue of obliterating the constitution was already a matter known to the trio of ministers, and that I probably had only been included as an afterthought.

"I have finished the proposal you asked me to draft, Your Excellency," the Constitutional Affairs Minister said, removing a thick folder from his briefcase. In it were kept the clean pages of his conjuring. He handed it over to the president and then reached for a glass of wine as though to thank himself for a good work done.

212

"This is the backbone of the plan. I think we all want to read it thoroughly and see what our able minister has given us here. This is supposed to be a highly classified document, gentlemen," the president refilled his glass obviously impressed with the thickness of the material.

The Justice Minister reached for both his glass of wine and the proposal lying on the president's table. He began to leaf through it. The Constitutional Affairs Minister had a copy in his hand and would raise his head occasionally from it to eye the president.

"You see, gentlemen, it's only now occurring to the opposition that it no longer has the power the white man left in its hands before we took it from them. You must all know it's at such moments your opponent becomes aware and begins to hatch funny ideas to hurt you, and you can see it in their faces."

When the Minister of Justice suggested that copies be made for all of us, the president nodded, and the minister quickly rose and volunteered to make the copies.

"We have a duty to this country, and I do not see why our goals can't be reached. The fantasy must be over by now. The opposition is out to bring us down by striking at our soft spots, you, gentlemen, could be the soft spots." The president rose from his chair and walked to the window. He lit a cigarette and puffed thick smoke into the air, but the air conditioner on the wall quickly dispersed it. "Lately I have compared the presidency to a doctor who smokes," he said, examining the cigarette in his hand. "The doctor carefully examines his cigarette-smoking patient and tells her that he has discovered that her lungs are filled with nicotine which will eventually kill her, yet the doctor is ready to light hundreds of sticks to fire up his own lungs even over the corpse of his patient.

"In politics there is the constant reminder of the phrase, 'self-preservation.' We are a young government in a young nation. I have people around me I believe are smart. Well, we owe it to each other to protect the presidency," he said.

The Justice Minister returned with copies of the proposal.

"The proposal, gentlemen, is our hope to prolonging our political journey. I definitely have no intention of sitting in this chair for a short while only to vacate it and become a dreamer. I intend to dream while sitting in it. We all have dreams for our country, but tell me what makes a dream a reality? Is it not when it is backed by power?"

The Minister of Internal Affairs agreed. He added something in a sheepish voice, but nobody heard what he said.

The president returned to his chair still holding his cigarette between his fingers. "Look at those fine young men, how they are destroying their future! What would make a man destroy himself? The people voted for us, but we must not forget that these same people can be turned against us. Every second of every minute, every minute of every hour, every hour of every day and every day of every year there is campaigning moment until the votes are counted, again and again."

Looking passed him under the table, I saw about a dozen empty bottles of wine. He had obviously been drinking before I entered his office.

I reached for the bottle of wine and filled my glass. Inside me, I became angrier every second of every moment. I examined the faces of his ministers wishing to know whether any of them had the integrity to think like I was thinking, of a president who milked his people, even his friends, and then dumped them afterward. However, they all seemed to be carrying the opportunistic look of deprived children, at least for as long as they were ministers under him.

I received a copy of the proposal, but the Justice Minister, in giving me a copy, stirred my anger even more. On returning to the room with the photocopies of the proposals, he had handed them over to us in order of our ranks. It was clear that he wanted to make a statement to me. He first returned the president's copy on the table, bowing like a court page, and then he gave the Constitutional Affairs Minister a copy, even though as the author he already had one. I was sitting close to him, but he ignored my outstretched hand and went on to give the Internal Affairs Minister a copy. He then turned around, examined his labor, satisfied that the essentials had been gratified before he shoved a copy before me without even turning to look at me.

I reached for my glass and tried to gulp my anger down, but I felt it bulging in my throat. I turned my attention to the proposal and examined its title, *Strategic Planning Proposal for a One Party State in Kaibara* . My glass

215

nearly slipped from my hand as I gasped for breath. I didn't agree with the first thought that came to my mind, that the presidency would be consolidated under the new scheme.

"Gentlemen, we are a team. God knows that I keep reflecting on that every day. I have a closed policy, which I have always shared with you. We are sure approaching our toughest challenge, converting Kaibara to a one party state!"

My heart pounded inside me like the hiccupping of a dog. Converting Kaibara to a one party state? I should not be at this meeting, no, not me to be a part of this evil plan. I recalled the conversation I had had with the American Ambassador. Had he got wind of the president's devilish plan? Was he, at our last meeting, trying to find a way of telling me about it? What did he want me to do?

At this point, the presidential spokesman walked into the room. As though he didn't notice us, he went directly to the president and whispered into his ear.

"Mr. Spokesman, could you share your news with these men? We all own this party, and we all have one mind. Let our voices like the morning sun rise as one."

The spokesman cleared his throat. "Hello, gentlemen, this is actually supposed to be a classified briefing, as the president had said, and must remain so for the next twenty-four hours." He looked at his watch. "Regarding the motion to introduce a one party system, I can safely say our chances are high. I have had audiences with disgruntled opposition members of parliament who have assured me they would defect by

216

the next parliamentary meeting which is twenty-four hours from now. It is no secret that with a defection of a considerable number, when the bill is mounted, parliament will just rubber-stamp it."

The ministers applauded.

"I have it down here, Mr. President!" the Constitutional Affairs Minister raised his hand like an eager schoolboy. "My proposal has divided the campaign into two: the direct mandate of the ordinary voters all over the country and the general consideration of parliament."

"And I am just thinking, Mr. President, that a people's convention largely of the rural populace will make our success as easy as saying it," the Justice Minister said.

"Your idea is *so* perfect!" the president was almost whistling it as he reached out to pat the minister on his back.

Crediting himself for what the president had just called "a perfect idea," the Justice Minister leaned back with all his teeth exposed as he hunched his shoulders.

I heard myself utter a loud cry of pain inside on discerning the scheme. Of the five hundred thousand people of RoMarong City, twenty percent of the voters were either educated or were exposed enough to read between the lines. Such a situation could serve a detrimental blow to the new conspiracy of a rubber stamp. The president and his team realized that their scheme would not be supported by RoMarong City's diversely educated metropolitan population. In addition, there was the broad international community under whose supervision any RoMarong City convention could take place. The team, therefore, decided to exploit the larger and uneducated population in the rural areas.

As the discussion continued, I flipped open several pages and my eyes ran over the line, "Objectives for a One Party State." The minister author had listed his objectives across the page cosmetic and conspiratorial:

(a) A one party state would strive to address national development via all its given potential within (but not limited to) the frame of our country's diversification, the multiethnic cultural aptitude of which has the potential of unifying the peoples of this country under an umbrella political philosophy, ideology, and characteristics;

(b) Given the small size of Kaibara both in geography and population, a country measuring 71, 740 square kilometers and its population being 3.6 million, multiparty politics has the tendency to create loopholes that cause waste of the nation's economic and natural resources and distract her children from the goals of nation building and deviating their minds into modes of unhealthy competition.

(c) Given the impressive structure of local traditional governments in Kaibara , from the paramount chiefs right through to chiefdom speakers and council members, the creation of political pluralism in central government is not only contradictory to tradition but renders this indigenous arrangement dysfunctional.

(d) In their move to create anarchy among African peoples, the British colonial masters, who themselves had no oppositions in the colony while they governed it, concocted multiparty pluralism so

that their rogues might return and milk our country while we butcher each other.

(e) It is no secret that the founding fathers of our independence decried the British colonial masters for their insistence on introducing multiparty pluralism. We, the inheritors of their untiring campaign, will only ensure that their spirits rest in peace when we achieve their dream of uniting the nation under a common symbol.

I shut the pamphlet and inwardly raged with fire. The first thought that came to my mind was to tear the proposal into shreds, toss it on the president's table, and walk out the door. But I hadn't forgotten his strength behind that door, his three letter acronymic militia with their hunger for molestation plainly visible in their bloodshot eyes.

I had still not forgotten how the president ordered his bodyguards to molest a senior party official who had visited State House to inquire as to why the president's promise to include his name on the list of cabinet ministers had not been honored. The president, of course, didn't have anything with which to compensate him, so he had summarily dismissed him from his presence. The man protested the dismissal more than he had protested the issue that had brought him to the House. The president took offense, and thought that this sort of behavior would continue in others unless he set an example. He ordered that the man be thrown out of his presence. The soldiers had taken his command literally. In one horrendous move, the man was gathered into a bundle, and the next minute he was flat on the ground at the foot of the three-story building. His ambition ended in a wheelchair.

"Mr. Johnson!" the President called my name again.

I was taken aback by his voice.

"Here is where you come in handy. Your special duty is to thoroughly read the proposal, make any necessary input, and endeavor to understand it as though you wrote it. Keep in touch directly with me," he paused and reached for his glass. "There doesn't seem much you are doing in that Southern African thing, so I want you to plan this whole exercise with me because you will be heading the nationwide committee I will be announcing in three days."

The ministers and the spokesman burst into a frenzy of laughter. They were obviously laughing with scorn at the reference of the president to my job. I felt mortified and disturbed at the same time. I remember there was a particular period when nothing happened in the party without the president first asking for my blessings. During that period, most of those who eventually became members of his cabinet where people who answered to me with a "yes sir."

"Do you mean *I* am to clean up this proposal and to monitor its implementation, Mr. President?" I spat fire. I was certain that his ministers and spokesman had caught my disdain, even if the president hadn't, or had he?

"It means, Mr. Johnson that all other assignments you have on your desk now become secondary to that proposal you are holding."

I hung the pamphlet in the air as though it had just materialized there. I could feel my anger creeping in me. I felt the eyes of the others on my skin in the ensuing quietness.

"Certainly sir, Mister President, certainly," I feared that my smile to the president would turn into contempt.

17

I angrily drove along the streets as I left the president's office. I hated his henchmen more than I had hated him. It appeared like I felt the ugly face of the president's spokesman injecting me with an asthmatic anger; the dirty laughter of the ministers appeared to be coming from my car radio.

I visualized my wife going round and round the phone at home, occasionally picking up the receiver to reassure herself that the phone was in working order. She might only have assumed that the meeting had degenerated into a drinking party. I knew I was supposed to have called her. She must have formed countless images of the president towering over me, congratulating his new minister.

The thought of how she would dash to the door on my arrival at home, plant a kiss on my lips, reach for my briefcase with the delicacy of a nurse, help me out of my inconvenient suit, settle me in the living room, and search my eyes for the good news that *was not just there,* frustrated me. She would search me all over, examining each line in my face, every small movement of muscle for signs of my success. Then, with her patience exhausted, she would fire off the cannonade of questions she'd been struggling to keep inside.

The evening was already too much for me to handle.

I just couldn't face my wife like that, only to tell her the president had offered me the bravest task in the land: to help Hercules carry the sky.

What a sick president!

What a sick world!

What a sick me!

I exited the main road named in honor of the president and drove on the side of the donor funded stadium also named in his honor. Entering the road, his dinosaurian and exaggerated photo hung with his banana-splitting macho smile. I recalled him telling me it was the very photo he loved to be displayed after I had suggested to him that his images be mounted everywhere in the city.

Below his ubiquitous photo were two empty spaces recently prepared by mandate of the first and second vice presidents, who had reasoned that their photos, under that of the president would complete the trinity of the government. Because I didn't consider the plan a proper one, I had secretly convinced the president to overrule the mandate. Those were the days when things were done as I 'commanded'.

I must have looked at his photo too long because as I was negotiating the curve, I almost hit a taxicab that veered sharply out of my way with a squeal of tires. The cab barely sideswiped my old Hillman, and the driver poked his head out to render a few invectives before giggling to his overloaded passengers.

I ignored him.

That was one reason I had so badly wanted to be a government minister. Like those buffaloes in the president's office always did, I could have used my power, hit that taxi, and received a standing ovation. In the first place, the taxi driver would not have failed to recognize me. I would have been chauffeur-driven or if I liked, self-driven in the latest model of a powerful German Benz that would be flying our foreign-designed Kaibara national flag. My driver or I would have disembarked the Benz in a grandiose manner and, in full view of the crowding citizens, ordered that the taxi driver be put in jail.

In my anger, I took the next exit and turned onto the narrow street that led to the house where M'balu lived with her mother. The two of them, and, indeed, a number of relatives, lived in a three-bedroom apartment, which I rented for them. M'balu was a junior schoolteacher who was left to fend for her mother after her father died of a disability long endured from the Burma war. Many years back, the British had drafted Kaibarans to help them quell Hitler's madness, which had spread into Burma. Five months into the war, M'balu's father had felt the rupture before the sound. A bomb had taken a toll on his limbs.

Inside her room, I told her straight to her face that the president had failed me again. I stopped short of telling her I had been marked to carry on with Hercules' task.

M'balu had a way of making me feel like a seasoned fighter. She had a way of making every Herculean task I had seem like an everyday activity. M'balu was wonderful, not only in words but also in touch.

She felt the political aberration frustrating every cell in my body. Rising from her bed, she exuviated the sheet from her body. The contours of her golden skin reflected the rays of the glowing bulb. Excesses of her sloped down into the muscles in her legs. At once she approached me and began to caress me. Her forceful breathing merged with mine to produce a syncopated duet.

I had my share of the apple of delight before it choked me. Like a tired serpent she dropped below me. Wedging her hands, she grabbed me.

With my eyes firmly shut, I threw my head back and heaved a huge sigh. Creeping backward and still glued to my body, she slowly hauled me to the bed where our forms intertwined. I reached to her soul.

"Go to sleep, baby, go to sleep," she ordered me in a spiritual tone. "You'll forget that there's an ungrateful world out there."

That was exactly what I did.

"Sir, the Constitutional Affairs Minister has called your direct line twice this morning," my secretary said with her head bowed. "He asked that you return his call as soon as you come in."

I had entered my office unable to look my staff in the eyes. I quickly went past their sympathetic greetings and murmured a reply. They had all noticed my excitement the previous day after the president had invited me to his office. In their little corner, I had heard them gossiping about their own excitement over the potential success of their beloved boss. I imagined how they must have clung to their radios, hoping to hear my appointment in the news. Had I been made a cabinet minister, I wouldn't have reported for work in the same office building the next day. Instead, I would have turned up at lunch hour to pack up my personal effects and vacate in time for my successor, if there would have been another. I remember having told my staff immediately after the elections that if I were moving anywhere as a cabinet minister, I would take all of them with me. The four of them—the secretary, the janitor, the messenger, and the driver—had served me since I co-owned a law firm.

After a while, during which time I had sat fixed in my chair letting my mind roam without pinning it on any particular issue, my secretary knocked on the door, something she never did. She had always walked in robust and unannounced. I invited her in. Our eyes met briefly, but she glanced quickly away, avoiding my gaze as though I had strictly warned her against it.

"In case, uh you wish to return the call….this is the telephone number of the minister." She dropped it on the table and quickly vanished behind the door.

I must have sat motionless for another five minutes before I rose and walked to the window. There was a silhouette above the brazen river in the open distance with the morphological characteristic of an amoeba. It seemed to be rising to a rain in the sky. Suddenly, dark clouds crept along like a cautious hunter. Within its watery muezzin, dragons barked with cylindrical fire bursting from their faces.

Then the phone rang.

It must have rung three times before I heard the urgent footsteps of the secretary approaching my door.

"That's your direct line, sir!" she said, her eyes wide open.

I must have growled at her because all at once I saw her back off, and my door creaked shut. Unaware of the scene, the phone kept ringing. It rang three more times and then stopped. When I turned to look outside, there was a heavy downpour. I could see vehicles moving up and down, school children, men, and women scurrying for shelter. The rain pelted hard on a fine people whose lives were secretly being planned for a conversion into a game park.

I shut my window and drew the blinds as the rain blew into my office. I returned to my desk and remembered to read the newspapers for that day. Most of the stories had to do with the police running down small time criminals caught stealing from merchants, rural land disputes and their fatal conclusions, and the mass migration of young men and women to the provincial town of Nokoh in search of diamonds.

None of the newspapers had a clue of the things being hatched. I began to imagine stories carrying my name in the newspapers as the dimwit who spearheaded the one-party gibberish. My face in black and white would be stuck on the front page. Then it would begin to appear in the inside pages, center spread in the form of cartoons. In these I would assume many postures in public platforms. In some, I would look like a gargoyle with my mouth wide open exposing poisonous canine teeth.

The phone rang again.

I imagined how uncomfortable my secretary must have felt, being frightened to do her job as she ought to do. I resolved to pick up the phone, partly to relieve her tension of not knowing what to do.

"Mr. Johnson, I left a message for you to return my call," the Constitutional Affairs Minister said.

"Oh did you? I must have been busy with other matters. How may I help you, Mr. Minister?"

It seemed that my addressing him as "Mr. Minister" went into his head and winded him.

"I wanted to discuss the issue of our meeting yesterday. You, of course, know what I am talking about."

"Ah, I guess so. What about it?"

"I suggested to the president this morning that since we are still working on a first draft, a raw document if you like, you can begin by first reporting whatever work you have done for me."

I must have cursed under my breath because I instantly became choked with anger.

"I don't understand you?" I said. I wanted to add his usual salutation but I cut out the *"Mr. Minister"* crap.

"Well, let me put it this way: I interpret the president's new assignment as making you answerable directly to me."

"Look, do you think you are talking to the right person?" It was my first reaction as my anger overcame me.

"Wait a minute. This is the Constitutional Affairs Minister on the line, Mr. Johnson?"

"Mr. Minister, you must know that I am still working in the presidential office. My official orders command me to be answerable to the president through his spokesman. And another thing, could you allow me time to read the proposal?" I took a deep breath. "I have yet to read the proposal that you only submitted yesterday."

There was a short pause before he responded. "Mr. Johnson, I have my opinion about you, which I am not prepared to say over the phone now!"

My anger exploded. "Well, Mr. Minister, I have a surprise for you! You are itching to boss me around, but I don't see why you believe you are capable." I thought of dropping the handset, but I held on to it.

"Mr. Johnson, it is no secret how envious you are of some of us. Well, prepare for this, it is not our fault that the president chose not to give you a cabinet position. Now looking at his decision again, I think he used his better judgment to throw you to a place as far away as Southern Africa!"

"Well, for your information," I fired back, "I have read the gibberish of what you chose to call a proposal. It is the most terrible piece of material I have ever seen in print. The president must have made you a minister in his sleep. And don't forget that I know what led to some of you to be compensated."

I heard his handset bang against the phone. Similarly, I slammed mine down and slouched in the chair as though I had just been withdrawn from a battlefront. Almost immediately, my door flew open and my secretary came dashing in.

"While you were on your line, the American Ambassador called and --."

"Get out of my sight! I don't care about a call even from God!" I chased her to the door and shut it after her.

18

The president arranged his face in an undecided expression as I entered his office. I knew of nothing that ever moved him. Once he told me everything under the sun, including making love, carried with it a political implication in which either partner hoped to steal the show. It was in recognition of that harsh reality he chose the glittering celestial beam as the party symbol. "We battle with it from scorching to soothing," he had said.

Already I was beginning to feel the burning rays of the sun.

He sat in his executive chair and spread his hands as though his dignity needed to be constantly gathered about. He looked past his three ministers who sat before him like below average students who required special counseling.

I walked past them and stretched my hand out to the president. Without taking it he directed me to an empty chair and leaned over the scattered papers on his mahogany table.

One of the ministers giggled as I withdrew my empty hand.

I eyed the Constitutional Affairs Minister, but I noticed he bowed his head perpetually over his lewd conception. The other ministers concentrated on the president. For a while, only the sound of the air conditioners could be heard within the claustrophobic four walls.

"Mr. Johnson, I understand you have a problem with the document the Constitutional Affairs Minister prepared for the creation of a one-party system?" the president said without raising his head.

It is you I have a problem with, Mr. Idiot! I thought of bursting out.

My second thought was how much more had the minister told the president? The spokesman entered and took a seat at the back of the office.

"Sir," I said. "When it has to do with creating an agenda for the implementation of the document, may I suggest, Mr. President, that the Constitutional Affairs Minister's department handles it exclusively?" I didn't know how else to tackle the issue. I was convinced by now that my days were numbered before the president.

"Mr. Johnson, we are talking here about classified information. You see, I have trusted your judgment and I am aware that your analysis can sure bring many a justification to the document. I am very positive that we will succeed in instituting a one-party system, but I want the concerted efforts of both you and the Constitutional Affairs Minister in this document to give it credence before it reaches the hands of donor nations and the Breton Woods Institutions. Besides, Mr. Johnson, don't you feel honored to be part of this history making moment?"

"In that case, Mr. President, I think a thorough document can only be put together after the conventions are held. We would be dealing with statistics and data that——."

At this point the president was up from his chair and was pacing about us. "Mr. Johnson, you don't understand. I see you don't understand," he turned to me. "We have been around long enough in this country to determine what the people want. What we want to do here is to use that knowledge of our people to develop a master document justifying the need for the change of this system to a workable one."

"Mr. President, are we here to develop a document for our own pleasure or for the pleasure of the ordinary many out there?" I dropped a bomb.

The president paused.

The ministers gaped at me in awe.

The presidential spokesman began to rise but sank back in his seat.

The president returned to his chair and cleared his throat.

"Let me put it this way, Mr. Johnson. We are suspending your current assignments on Southern Africa and your office will be attached to that of the

Ministry of Constitutional Affairs. You will offer the minister all the help he needs in the making of the document."

Why was the president using the "We" pronoun? Was it a struggle between them and me? A burning anger and madness took control of me. I was shaking inside with rage. My throat itched, and my collar burnt around my neck. I must say that with all my insubordination, I was taken aback by the calmness of the president.

"It was a reasonable suggestion that I called Mr. Johnson to discuss on the phone yesterday, Mr. President," said the Constitutional Affairs Minister. "And I believe the two of us are capable of producing the kind of document you would like to see."

"I'm offering to help in the making of the document if it pleases the president," the Judiciary Minister said.

"Three hands make the work lighter," said the president, "but because I want the document to have a name value, Mr. Johnson will head a committee of a long list of names, which will carry an evidence of nationwide contribution to its making."

"Mr. President," I cleared my throat. "With due respect to the honor, I would not care to perform any state duty under this Minister of Constitutional Affairs. And what's more, Mr. President, after turning it over in my mind the whole of yesterday, I believe the attempt to convert Kaibara to a one-party state is a plan that has arisen from bad advice given to your office."

I shut my eyes and waited for the bombs to drop on me. I waited for the blows and kicks of the bodyguards. However, none came, and when I opened my eyes again, those of the president, the ministers, and the presidential spokesman were staring at me as though Armageddon had just been announced and had passed without incidence.

"Mr. Johnson needs a rest, gentlemen," the president said, laughing. Everyone else stared in disbelief. The prolonged laughter of the president rang inside his office as he pounded his desk. He leaned backward in his chair, then surged forward, and slapped his desk again. His laughter filled the room; his eyes filled with tears. The ministers took their cue in turns and then the spokesman. It held for a while before I joined in.

I felt the weight of the embarrassment I had caused him before the eyes of his ministers, but why had he laughed so hard? It was really that he was crying, I guess. He was certainly going to come after me. My heart pounded at the thought. I knew he was not going to treat my insubordination lightly. He would want to deal with me to impress upon his ministers that he was a no-nonsense leader.

I feared he had already called my house a hundred times to tell me how much I had disappointed him. If that would be just about it, then it would not look all that bad.

M'balu crossed my mind, and I soon began imagining her pleasantness. I drove my car to her house.

Ignorant of the imbroglio I had created for the president, M'balu had charged me at her room entrance accusing me of coming from another woman. She began to beat against my chest saying she'd had to

235

endure my wife, and now I had begun cheating with another woman. Lost in the island of my worries, I considered her berating a disturbance of the spirit, and so I delivered a slap across her face. How could she not know she too was a cheat? Pouncing on me like a lion, she began to wrestle me. She tore my shirt as I pulled her by her hair. She kicked me in my groin, and I saw stars. With one blow, I sent her writhing on the bed.

Her mother dashed into the room and separated us. An hour later, M'balu and I embraced as we both bitterly cried over each other's shoulder.

When I went to sleep, I had a terrible dream. I was running through thick woods. The night was black, and the thunder cracked with occasional wiry lightening above. I heard footsteps advancing behind me. In fact, they were the steps that had sent me running. I didn't know where I was coming from or where I was headed. It seemed to me I had been running for a long time.

I realized that while I stumbled on stumps and creeping plants, the footsteps behind me moved across the ground with the ease of familiarity. I tried looking back each time the lightning struck, but I was unable to make out any image. Just then there appeared a wide valley before me. From afar, I could hear the waterfall. It also seemed the footsteps had gotten closer to me. Suddenly, I tripped against a stump and stumbled, but instead of falling, I flew in the air above the valley!

I woke with perspiration all over me and breathing as if I had actually been running. Fear swept over me. I looked at my watch and noticed that it was just the small hours of the night. Outside I could hear the noise of people conversing in raised voices. M'balu was not in the room.

"The president!"

It was the first word I had uttered. I got up and searched in my wallet for the number, and I reached for M'balu's phone.

"Residence of the—may I help you?" I noticed the incompleteness in the salutation.

"My name is Desmond. May I speak to the Ambassador?"

I was asked to wait. I felt like I waited forever before the American accent came through.

"Desmond! Thanks for calling me. Are you calling to tell me about the coup attempt that has just been announced?"

"Coup!" I could not believe what I was hearing.

"Oh, you have not heard? Fifteen military officers just tried to overthrow your president. But they have been arrested," the Ambassador said.

"I am just getting to know this right now," I will find out more and keep you informed.

"Yes, please do. I especially would like to know about the coup plotters"

I hung up and reached for the bedside radio. .

It was an unbearably hot summer in New York. The wind sweated and blew watery air across the landscape. A brutal fragrance rose to the skies of New York taking back the beige atmosphere of the winter that had embraced the rocks and waters with a perpetual emotional relationship. But the flowers of summer were forever wild, breaking forth on the hills of the parks and melting in the rivers of water. Warm life was everywhere on the landscape, the forested buildings flung their shadows against each other, and people emerged from their cocoons complementing the bold expression of the new season.

The sun worked its way into my skin because I was loosely dressed in shorts and a T-shirt. My sneakers were brand new. But for Yolanda, I'd still be clad in one of my out-of-fashion French suits. In my recreational outfit, I felt lighter and younger. New York City had many exciting outfits. Women in particular did not cease to astound me with their semi-nudity. The sin of lust possessed every New Yorker. It was in this atmosphere I was when I showed up for that evening English class.

Drenched in sweat, I arrived at the home of the Mexican couple. Barbara welcomed me at the door. After I'd sat down, she brought me cold water in a glass, which I drained in one gulp. I waved off the offer of a second glass because already the cool air by the AC was fusing with the quenching chill of the water within me. Fernando and Chernobyl sat opposite each other staring at me as though I had just landed from space.

"Maybe I'm in the wrong house if these two guys don't know me," I said turning to Barbara.

Fernando laughed out loud, "We know you. We just think you look great, like a young boy!"

"Well, I have a daughter who thinks I'm not growing older," I said.

"I don't blame her," Barbara said, returning from the kitchen.

It was at this time I was alarmed by the number of big whiskey bottles under the dining table. The two men raised their glasses and said almost at once, "Welcome to a no-learning day!"

I settled into a chair nearby and proceeded to show admiration at the number of bottles they had downed. Chernobyl reached for a glass and handed it to me.

"Kill yourself, teacher!"

I said thanks and reached for the whiskey he was passing to me. I poured a little and looked through the prism of the burgundy liquid. I shut my eyes and gulped. It had been two years since I drank anything this strong. I felt my throat pulsing with pain as the harsh liquid burned the flesh. A somber feeling crept all over me, and I rested well on the loveseat.

"The first shot is the best. That's what we say in the Ukraine," Chernobyl said laughing.

"And in Mexico, the last shot is never remembered," Fernando threw in.

We all laughed out loud. I poured some more and proceeded to sip it slowly. Already I was enjoying both the company and the whiskey.

"Certainly, it didn't look like we would have a class anyway," I said, pointing to the empty bottles under the table.

"Not very sure about that," Barbara put in.

"Well, what are you waiting for, Barbara? Join us," said Chernobyl as he waved his hand.

"I prefer orange juice," she said raising her glass hidden behind her back.

"I keep telling you juice is for kids," Fernando said filling his glass.

I don't remember how long we were there drinking, but when I looked at my watch it was past four. By this time, both Fernando and Chernobyl were snoring. I tried to wake them up, but they were as still as a stone. I took two more glasses. I didn't know what else to do. I was already feeling the embarrassing silence hanging between myself and Barbara, who didn't care to wake the two men sprawling in the living room. Sitting opposite me, she was just smiling occasionally and sipping her juice, which had been the only glass she'd had since I entered the house. Eventually I said thanks to Barbara and bade her goodbye. When I rose, I felt a heavy pang of pain in my head, and I was forced to drop down again at the chair.

"Are you okay, Mr. Johnson?" Barbara asked rushing to my chair.

"I'm fine, I'm fine. It's just that I'd not drunken this stuff for so long now."

"Oh, I'm sorry. Why do they have to let you drink it?" she said like a mother looking after a wounded child.

I felt the fragrance of the French perfume she wore coming from her body. I raised my head up to allow a distance between the two of us. She went for a glass of cold water and quickly returned from the kitchen.

"Here, drink this. It will help to make you better soon."

I took the glass, drank from it, and thanked her.

"Maybe I should be going at once," I said.

"They have been drinking all day," she said of her husband and Chernobyl.

"I have to go now," I said getting up and walking to the door.

"Are you driving? You think you can make it to your place?"

She was convinced I was either too drunk or extremely upset, but I needed only to be left alone to recuperate. As I reached for the door, she coughed and halted me.

"Maybe I should drive you home, Mr. Johnson."

"*Nah*, I don't think you should worry about that," I said.

"No, no, it's fine with me. These men won't get up even if I should go to Mexico a whole day and come back tomorrow."

"Well, if it is not a problem with you, I could do with a ride half way through my journey."

She quickly disappeared into a room and came out changed into jeans and T-shirt. The two men continued to snore out a duet of bad jazz. Fernando had his head thrown back on the sofa and his hand lay on the knee of Chernobyl whose mouth was wide open. Barbara unplugged all electrical appliances before we stepped outside. The sun still hung in the sky, journeying slowly westward. The streets blazed with activities and traffic was moving faster than usual. Barbara and I spoke not a word until we arrived where I asked her to drop me. I assured her I could make the rest of my journey home, for I was feeling good then.

"Summer is too short a season; I want to enjoy it," I said.

Suddenly a painful expression crossed her face. I repeated myself, but she still didn't answer back. She was staring directly at the dashboard.

"What? Is something the matter with you or the car?" I asked.

"Oh, no, no, I'm fine. Did you say you want to get out here?"

"Yes, I—I can get out here," I reached my hand for the door as the car came to a halt.

"Mr. Johnson?"

I turned around.

"It's about Fernando," she began, her head down.

"What, is he in some kind of a trouble?" I was afraid she would ask me to represent her husband in court. I'd never practiced law in America. After I was told I needed to return to American schools if I wanted to practice law in the country, I abandoned the effort. After all, I convinced myself I was not in exile forever and that I was soon going back to RoMarong City where I'd started making a name for myself. Thirty years later I was still only a lawyer on paper.

Turning to me with deeply troubled eyes, she said, "Fernando does not care about my body."

"What happened to your body? Are you sick?"

She again looked into my eyes. "Fernando drinks a lot; he drinks every day." She paused and wiped the tears trickling down her face. "He always comes home drunk every day and sleeps like a dead man. I have had to put up with this since we came to this country. He does not

242

touch me. Chernobyl always comes home with him, and they end up sprawling on the living room floor dead just as we left them."

Wetness suddenly came to my lips. My heart leaped like the hind legs of a tiger. The whiskey I'd drunk washed over me like the forceful waters of the ocean. All throughout this time a deep silence engulfed us. When my tongue loosened, I turned to her and stammered with a fragmented voice that I was sorry for her. I noticed that her eyes were heavy with pain. Her beautiful face was blank and empty. I didn't realize that our eyes had held each other's for what seemed like forever. I suddenly reached for her as with an equal force I saw her reach for me. I felt tiny stars winking in my head as we pressed our lips together in a fervent, starving kiss. We sustained it for a long minute as I massaged her, searching for the pain all over her. I could see she felt like someone whose thirst had just been quenched. Groaning, she ate my mouth.

"Where do you live?" she fumbled for her car keys in the ignition and gunned the car down the road.

19

Bundeh Kargbo lived in a condominium at the edge of Manhattan. He was very happy to have both Amara and me over for dinner. Amara had relocated to New York to start his doctorate degree and had rented an apartment somewhere downtown. Our meeting at Bundeh's home was the second time the three of us had come together. On another day Bundeh had taken us to some nightclub where we spent the night looking at girls dancing in the nude.

We agreed to meet again at Bundeh's. He had a big wife with tremendous buttocks. She had a high enthusiasm for entertaining her guests. Bundeh had loaded his freezer with beers. There was pepper soup and several different African dishes.

"A chicken this size is hard to find in Kaibara today," Amara said with a mouthful.

"Well, what with the war and all that ignoring attitude of the outside world, whoever has time to rear a chicken properly?"

Bundeh raised his head from the big bite on his fork and laughed out loud, "The Americans, of course," he said. "Have you ever tasted a delicious chicken in this part of the world? A chicken like this I'm eating now was not originally a big one. It was fattened with all kinds of chemicals," he said. "Is it not from this kind of foods that we contract cancer and AIDS? Over to you, Mr. Scientist."

"I'll have to check that out, but no one has ever established that yet," Amara said laughing.

"You think corporate America get time to cross check something like that?" Bundeh said. "You are crazy! You know how much money they've got to lose. Is the human race not going mad with the mad cow disease all because the corporate world them the down play the whole thing?"

"I suspect the disease has gone to our politicians' heads with this political malapropism taking place in the continent," I said, opening the beer Bundeh's wife served me. "You remember the time of slavery, the white man carried pipes and gun powder for the African kings. That gunpowder went to the heads of the kings, and they began to sell Africans like crazy. The same thing the happen now. All this experiment for which Africans are guinea pigs, they make all man go crazy."

"That is deep thinking, Mr. Johnson, but I go get for cross check it in the laboratory," Amara said.

"Laboratory! Which laboratory? You think the white man is going carry you into every room in the laboratory? Them go make quick quick, and give you one lie lie PhD and send you back to Africa."

"No, that's not true. I go into every laboratory, any place the American student the go into in the laboratory," Amara vehemently protested.

"Even when you sleep in the night? Tell me, because it is that time they go in the lab and concoct their herbs full of AIDS, mad cow disease, and Ebola, carve them like lollipop, and ship them to our countries as charity," Bundeh said.

We all laughed long and loud. At this time, Bundeh's wife was stacking more drinks for us in the freezer. The latest Kaibara music was blasting the speakers as the summer sun brightened the day. The AC too was comforting us. Between Amara and me, a dozen green bottles lay dead. The conversation drifted to the negative reporting we believed the American television was committed to selling to the American audience. We wondered why there was hardly any mention of the achievements of the ECOMOG military force, for instance, that was currently busy helping to restore true democracy in the countries of Kaibara and and its neighbors.

"Is it not democracy these people stand for?" I asked.

"What do you expect?" Bundeh said. "Anytime that the American not be in front in international affair, don't bother; they never go support the good things initiated by others, let alone such idea the come out from Africa, *agbo*! They always provoke that idea, like

246

say it is rubbish. But once them get one intervention in a country where them get interest, them go use all that initiative and begin for publish them bogus volume praising themselves with other people them ideas."

"We've got to wake up and take the affair of the African continent into our own hands," thundered Amara.

"Affairs of what continent? Begin first with the simple demonstration which for happen in Washington, DC," Bundeh replied.

"Whatever happened with that demonstration?" I put in.

"That demonstration done sag under tribalism, my friend," Bundeh gulped his beer then continued. "The organization done divided the demonstrators into our many ethnic groupings. Mende in the left, Themne in the right, Krio in the middle, Limba in the corner and all other get them own small, small corner."

"Africa, my Africa!" Amara lamented with the beer pressed between his hands.

Suddenly the poet, David Diop, came to mind, a poet who became famous for the poem from which Amara had quoted the first line. I thought about the loss of many visionary Africans: Nkrumah, Lumumba, Senghor, and a host of others, and I began to wonder whether many years down the road, the growing illiteracy in the continent was to always be the curse of the continent. That evening, I learned that the demonstration to the White House hadn't taken place because the committee was still undecided on what positin of the war to present as a group.

247

Amara was already visibly drunk and was touching on every topic without allowing us to have our own say. He returned to the topic of his PhD not being inferior to those earned by white people. He denied not having access to every corner of any university laboratory. He said if he was not earning any serious education, how come he was being asked to teach classes at undergraduate levels to prepare white students? We were getting confused with his erratic blabbering and wanted him to stop jabbering.

"I think you need for take it easy now, my friend, and stop the drinking," I told him.

Then a wave of chorus came through the windows!

It was Amara who first heard the singing. He leaped from his chair and went to the window. He was not at first sure what it was, so he stood there attentively.

"Did you hear that?" he turned to me and asked.

"Hear what, your silence at the window?" Bundeh questioned.

"You guys better come and listen to this," Amara said.

"What, dog done cut your ears?" Bundeh said as he disappeared into his room.

I walked to where Amara was standing. It was then that the wind brought to us the loud echo of the song. I could actually feel the army of voices advancing. However, what astounded us, including Bundeh and his wife who had come to the window, was the fact that the song was in Krio on the streets of New York. Although we were convinced that only Kaibarans could be singing that song, we still couldn't imagine Kaibarans

taking to the orderly streets of New York singing
derogatory songs such as we were hearing.

> *Tiday na for me*
> *yesterday na you turn*
> *you nor do natin;*
> *way fowl young e nor*
> *pull teeth, nor to way*
> *e old e go pull am.*

> *Monkey nor go lef*
> *e black hand;*
> *lek wae dog eye the run blood*
> *na me time for kill all them bella.*

At once a set of other people were marching and
signing from the opposite direction, apparently in
opposition to the demands for which the first group
was marching. One group was extoling the government
officials in Kaibara while the other group was
presenting them as war-like, murderous and heartless
villains. In a space of five minutes the numbers of the
two groups were swelling into thousands. Or was it I
the one drunk enough to maintain a correct vision? I
suddenly found myself rushing to the door, and running
between the two crowds. What my motivation was, I
was not sure. As I ran into the middle, I began to feel
like I was returning into a dream I had had before—of
ten thousand children on one side of me, and ten
thousand others on the other side pulling the other side
of me. I lost focus, vision and consciousness!

249

I woke up in the middle of the night on the floor in my apartment. A sharp pain went across my face like lightening. Nothing came to my mind clearly about the number of beers the three of us gulped at Bundeh's. Was it last night or the previous night or a few days ago? In the meantime, I dragged myself to the water faucet, drew a glass of water, and gulped it down with two aspirins. It was then it all came back to me. I gasped, "Oh my God!" I quickly reached for my phone and called Bundeh. The line was busy. It was then I remembered that I hadn't returned home on my own. I didn't still know what to think about the night before and how I had got drunk and followed after the demonstrators up the road. This was madness, the very madness happening in my country, Kaibara. I began to connect my dream of children and the reality of Kaibarans singing in the street of New York City and how I had found myself in the middle of a double complexity.

I felt that my world was forever lost in exile! I staggered from the sink to the loveseat. My hands fell on crisp papers: the mail. I had not read my mail, I believe, for days. There were more than ten envelopes in the chair. They were mostly bills though. Then there was one with non-American set of stamps. It was the first mail I was to receive from RoMarong City! Who was this? I quickly tore it and opened the short letter. It was from M'balu!

"Desmond, I received the letter you sent from America. I didn't expect to hear from you after such a long parting. Your letter is

250

so loaded that I have the feeling that after the death of Archibald, you had no one to give you information about Kaibara. Well, I am myself a very unlikely source of information regarding many of the people you are asking about. It seems as if the rumors of the civil war coming to RoMarong have made many people to pack and go anywhere, in search of peace. Thank you for asking after me. I am good in health although I am not growing anymore younger as you used to say."

"My God! My M'balu is doing well!" I gasped as I bowed my head over the letter. I had feared the possibility that anything bad could have happened to M'balu ever since my family abandoned me.

"I am very grateful to be alive though in this country where madness itself has put on a human flesh and is roaming the streets seeking to destroy every expression of human civilization. You may know by now that the war has advanced as far as Nonkoh and already we in RoMarong are beginning to experience its effects. The capital is hunted daily by the presence of roadblocks and the military taking over the streets at night, I have to say I look terror in the face on a daily basis, and I no longer fear it. My love for you was seating in my heart all these years, until recently when it moved to my head. I do not anymore think it is mine even though I look up the road it ever should come walking along it"

I dropped the letter and wept in joy. I felt my heart yearning for the sight of M'balu. However, the migraine in my head boiled like a volcano. My mouth went dry. I felt a thunderous rain dropping in my heart. It was as though the whole world had squeezed into me and was now expanding to burst open inside. I was nauseated. My head twirled as if the end of the world had just begun inside of it.

I am hoping that you have grown up children now. How is my mate doing? Ahahaha...your letter brought back happy memories. Don't forget to send me money in your next letter. I have my niece by me who writes my letters. She hear stories of you all the time from me. Until I hear again from you, stay blessed.

Outside my room, I knew that New York was busy producing more gays, gun-toting youth, boxed homeless, pedestrian prostitutes, and all kinds of people. I tried not to think about my family as I want to think only of M'balu. I must have lost consciousness moments later, for when I came back around, I found myself in the couch with my head resting on a thick wad of pillows and Yolanda, staring at me.

"Oh, Dad! Are you feeling okay now?"

"Yes, I am. What happened to me?" I attempted to rise from the chair.

"Dad, why don't you just lie down for a while?"

"I'm sure I'm fine. Listen, after all of these, I've been meaning to let you know that I left my heart in Kaibara, and I should just go back there."

Just then I saw my estranged wife beside the window. She was looking out of the window as if nothing else was going on around her.

"Are you okay?" Yolanda asked.

In that instant, her mother went into the kitchen and returned with a cup of tea.

A knock at the door and Yolanda volunteered to answer it. She dashed to it, but almost immediately the door flew open and in came Barbara

"Are you sure you are in the right place?" Yolanda thundered.

"It's okay, Yolanda.

What is Barbara doing here! Not at this time, oh dear!

Just as though none of the others existed, Barbara dashed to me and felt for my head and asked whether I was doing okay.

I answered in the affirmative.

"Daddy, who is this?" Yolanda questioned.

"I am coming to that, Yolanda."

"I'm waiting." Yolanda stood at ease.

"Haven't you also seen his love letter from his *dear* from RoMarong City as well? I am out of here!"

I forced myself to stand up, but my head was spinning, and as I collapsed back into the chair, Barbara cupped me in her arms and laid me gently in the chair.

My wife gunned her way out of the door, and Yolanda mechanically chased after her.

After a while I gathered strength to demand of Barbara what she was doing in my house without a prior notice, but she would not have me bother myself with those concerns in the middle of the migraine eating into me. I realized that I was instantly in a mess already deeper than that which had divided my body and soul between home and exile.

20

Chernobyl arrived at my house that evening announcing his name even before reaching my door. The first thought that came to me was that he was probably followed closely by Fernando. Barbara had probably told them that I had had an affair with her. Chernobyl called out my name again. I could sense the liquor belching itself from his throat. The noise died down and so did my fear. From the couch I enquired who it was visiting without a prior notice.

"Your student, Lawyer Johnson. Me, Chernobyl. Sorry not told you I coming to see you."

"You should have called, Chernobyl. Are you alone?"

"Me alone, Lawyer Johnson, me alone."

"Cut that lawyer crap, Chernobyl."

He sent a rippling laughter into my tired ears. If it was not to warn me about Fernando I hoped he had not showed up hoping that I had time to share liquor with him. I pleaded with him to give me a minute to come to the door. I looked around me everything was neatly in order courtesy of Barabara who had straightened everything after our lovemaking. I let him in. It was the first time he was entering my apartment; but that did not stop him from making himself comfortable in my couch as soon as I let him.

"Mr. Johnson you don't know nothing about me, "he said.

I agreed without knowing where this was going. I still had an apprehension that Fernando had sent him to tell me he was going to kill me that day. *Does my wife have a hand in this?* I wondered.

"I have a letter for you," Chernobyl cut through my thoughts.

"Letter, who gave you a letter for me?" I asked.

Without responding, he removed an envelope from his pocket and, with a serious face, handed it to me. "This is going to surprise you," he said.

"My mind missed a beat. Could it be that Fernando is suing me for having an affair with his wife?" I looked at Chernobyl wide-eyed, but he refused to be moved into saying something to that effect. I moved to the window and quickly tore the envelop open. It was a letter from Kaibara. I turned to Chernobyl whose eyes where all over me. "How come you are receiving a letter from Kaibara on my behalf?"

Even though I was looking at the letter I wasn't concentrating on the contents. I kept asking myself how Chernobyl became the bearer of a letter to me from Kaibara.

"Me received it over the weekend," he said walking up to me. You see who wrote it to you?"

It was then that I looked below the page and saw the name of Borbor Pain. *What!* The Kaibara rebel leader? I chocked again and sighed. It was as if my legs were going off me. I headed for a chair and sat in it. Chernobyl had no impression in his face.

"Me know you are surprised, but read the letter first," he admonished like a little child. Diligently, I returned to the letter.

Barrister and Solicitor Desmond Johnson don't be surprised to receive this letter from your countryman and freedom fighter, Corporal Borbor Pain. I am holding on with the struggle to remove the cancer we have in RoMarong City calling itself a government. I have been told how strongly you feel about this matter. All of what is happening today was foretold long time ago. In fact, I will not be wrong to say that some of you people began this revolution even before some of us took up arms against the government. Your contribution to sustain democracy in Kaibara is written in the hearts of patriotic Kaibarans. My brother and comrade this struggle is not Borbor Pain's struggle. It is a Kaibaran struggle.

By this letter, I am extending an invitation to you, brother, to join me in this struggle, to continue to play that role you always wanted to play in the '60s that role for which you were chased into exile. The bearer of this letter will tell you how to contact me. I am on wire twenty-fours of the day talking to all parts of the world.

*You may have heard that there has been a successful military
coup in RoMarong City—that city that was waiting for me and I
supposed for you as well. The military is not the right force to
dislodge the thirty year gargantuan political mess that had
imprisoned our people. In fact, the military is an extension of the
political class. By every means, they too must be dislodged!*

I raised my head and met the scrutinizing eyes of
Chernobyl. "I don't understand, how do you feature in
all of this?"

"Me expected that question," he laughed. His face
was serious. He didn't look anything like the Chernobyl
I knew as my learner. "Me used to be a mercenary
fighter for the Corporal in Kaibara, but I only be with
him for six months before he allowed me to come
America."

"Wao, aren't you a hard nut? I'll be damned. You
have a whole explaining to do," I told him.

I got up and went to the kitchen and a few minutes
later, I returned with a bottle of Campari. Chernobyl's
face lit up and he muttered something unintelligible.
He accepted a glass from me. I opened and poured for
him. He stood up and walked to the window as he
drained his whole glass.

"Kill yourself," I told him.

He reached for the bottle and refilled his glass.

"Eighteen months. I will never forget that chapter of
my life. Me fought in the jungles of Kaibara for six
months as a mercenary. Two hundred and fifty of us
Ukrainians; but me and another Ukrainian were lucky to
find some diamonds, so we stopped fighting."

"How could he have allowed you to leave with the diamond and still maintain a relationship with you?" I asked him.

"We gave him a big diamond. Not a man you can double cross. He put me and my friend under gun point to give him more diamonds. But after a while he trusted us and let us go," he said as he refilled his glass.

"And so you lost the diamond?"

"Nope, we had more diamonds.

Chernobyl gulped his glass and looked at me in the eye, "No way, we stayed but we didn't have to fight no more." He refilled his glass. He was going on it way faster than me. "He made us emissaries. That's how I came to America and the other Ukrainian to Europe and Asia." He walked up to me. "Lawyer Johnson, Borbor Pain wants you and wants you and wants you to help him in this fight." Returning to the window, he added, "He told me he knows about you, and I only helped him trace you. Then he dig and dig and dig and found out who you are."

"His rebels amputated the feet of my…my…loved one."

Chernobyl almost immediately cut in, "Your girlfriend, Vanessa."

Instant hurt cut across my heart. "How do you know that? How do you know her? Have you been spying on me?"

I then realized that Yolanda could be too difficult to understand.

"No, Lawyer Johnson, another thing I want to tell you is that your daughter and I are close friends. I learned that from your daughter who is worried about you."

I rose from my chair with the gradual fierceness of a lion. And with a finger pointed at his face, I stammered, "If I ever...ever...ever...ca...tch you near to my family again...If I ever, I will kill you with my hands."

He began to say something. But by now my anger had taken over the vision in my eyes.

"Get out of my house...now! I will not hear any more from you...get out."

He looked deeply into my eyes, probably to see the depth of my anger. He then raised his glass and drained the liquor down his throat. Licking his mouth, he walked to the table near him and stood the glass. All the while I stood firmly like a stature watching him. We met eyes. He walked to the door and disappeared into it. I fell into the couch and bowed my head, sighing.

At once too many matters crowded themselves in my head. I wanted to know to what extent my daughter and Chernobyl were related; to what extent Borbor Pain needed me. I however realized that the man who held the answers to my questions was the man I just drove away from my apartment. The thought was stuck in me like a headache. I reached for the liquor and it was then I realized that Chernobyl had almost finished it. What was left couldn't touch the bottom of a glass, so I gulped from the bottle; and when the content was quickly finished, I smashed the bottle on the wall, got up and repeatedly rendered the chair I sat in several kicks before I overturned the table near me. I threw myself in the couch again and closed my eyes. M'balu's name flashed on my mind, and in that instant the phone rang. I allowed it to ring forever and only reached for the handset when it felt as if the ringing would not stop.

The caller announced himself.

It was Borbor Pain!

"A bad time to call?"

"A terrible *time* to call. Someone needs to explain to me what is going on here," I demanded.

"I don't know what is going on your end, but there is a war going on my end, and I'm trying to win it by winning you over," Borbor Pain answered.

"Listen, thanks, but I have been at war since my exile started thirty years ago," I told him.

"My dear brother, no one fights a war in exile. You hit at the wrong target," Borbor Pain countered. "Exile has a way of making someone like you a complete foreigner to the original home," he added. "You must try to rescue yourself, Mr. Johnson. You have been at war all these thirty years, but that war has been one in which you have been busy beating on your chest in a foreign land. You must have learned a lot now that it doesn't really yield any fruits to keep blaming it on your intellect that you could have taken up the gun and shoot the dictators in Freetown right between their eyes. You didn't do it, and I know all these thirty years you have felt guilty that you betrayed the people of Kaibara...and...now..."

"But you were the one who ran away when Kaibara needed you most," Borbor Pain said.

"I didn't run away, I was chased out!" I shouted immediately he ended his words.

"Kaibara didn't chase you away, remember?" Borbor Pain reasoned.

I immediately cut in, "If you should know, I was a victim of the Kaibara you are invoking right now. A Kaibara that jumped and rested all its weight on my small frame. You were busy cleaning up your old guns to fight new and complex causes the wrong ways."

I grew an immediate anger at the thought that my life has always been subjected to being a rogue follower to rogue leadership. There was that man who later became the first president of Kaibara wooing me to join his political party. I had jumped for it in less than three seconds of inviting me, and look at how it all ended, how I had to be the one running away from him. Yes, I certainly ran away from him, and not from Kaibara. When I thought about it deeply, I felt like a fool who had all the chances of staying back and defending my claim to Kaibara. But I allowed that rogue to chase me out of my country. Thirty years later, I knew it would never be the same again. I knew I had lost it. And now if I must gain, at least, my dignity, I had to be on the telephone listening to another rogue trying to invite me to join his rebel movement.

"Mr. Johnson, I want to invite you to come with me on the road to Kaibara. There are men in military fatigue you and I need to drive out away from RoMarong. Not even a coup has changed the players

261

down in RoMarong. The boys down there pretending to run the show are the very children of the big daddies who sent both you and I into exile. They are chicken who went home to roost. The real deal is between you and I."

I chuckled and heaved a sigh of relief. M'balu crossed my mind again. My nagging wife came to mind. My daughter's affiliation with Chernobyl came to mind. I felt explicitly broken. It seemed to me that both my home and my exile had created an embarrassment I had to avoid facing; but at the same time home and away remained the only two choices if I was ever to move on. A sudden surge of abhorrence for exile came over me and I felt the fear of confronting the man whose wife I had taken to bed, the woman who had separated from me, and the messenger who had befriended my daughter in a rather dubious manner.

"Thanks for the invite. After thirty years in exile, I am on the road to Kaibara with you as from today," I bellowed in the mouth piece.

"Well, we had better gotten you started on your journey. *Becoming a devil before becoming an angel* is the only way to make the foundation for a lasting democracy in Kaibara."

Printed in the United States
By Bookmasters